To my sister, Dana, for when we're together again.

AB

To my parents, for always encouraging me to explore my imagination.

RD

MOONCHILD

City of the Sun

AISHA BUSHBY

Illustrcted by Rachael Dean

Farshore

Farshore

First published in Great Britain 2021 by Farshore
An imprint of HarperCollins*Publishers*
1 London Bridge Street, London SE1 9GF
farshore.co.uk

HarperCollins*Publishers*
1st Floor, Watermarque Building, Ringsend Road
Dublin 4, Ireland

Text copyright © Aisha Bushby 2021
Illustrations copyright © Rachael Dean 2021
Aisha Bushby and Rachael Dean have asserted their moral rights.

ISBN 978 0 7555 0062 8
Printed and bound in Great Britain by CPI Group
1

A CIP catalogue record for this title is available from the British Library.

Stay safe online. Any website addresses listed in this book are correct at the time
of going to print. However, Farshore is not responsible for content hosted by
third parties. Please be aware that online content can be subject to change
and websites can contain content that is unsuitable for children.
We advise that all children are supervised when using the internet.

MIX
Paper from
responsible sources
FSC™ C007454

This book is produced from independently certified FSC™ paper
to ensure responsible forest management.

For more information visit: www.harpercollins.co.uk/green

The Three Moonchildren, the Stormbird and the curse

It is said to have happened, some moons ago, that three children and their *jinn* went on a perilous voyage in search of a cursed city covered entirely in brass. The trees were covered in brass, as were the houses, and the palace that stood tall in the middle of the island. And, perhaps the most peculiar thing of all, the people were covered in brass too.

The city was called Alhitan, and it was not easy to find. It required stealth, cleverness, and a dash of danger. Because it stood in the depths of the ocean, on the back of a singing whale. A whale that rose only during the blood moon.

Why? you ask. Why would three children and their *jinn* take such a journey?

Well, I'll tell you.

But first it might be an idea to tell you a little about *jinn* . . .

For those who might not know (and I'll make allowances, even though you should know by now), *jinn* exist at the very edges of our realm. They exist in a place most people don't think to look: the place where we hold our emotions. Children who welcome the *jinn*, who can name them as a companion, have access to this realm. And they call themselves Moonchildren.

Moonchildren, as the name might suggest, gather their magic from the moon, with their *jinn* acting as a vessel. Like the tides, the Moonchildren are guided by the moon, led by her, and together they share a bond that can't be broken.

But be warned, because not all *jinn* are paired to a human. And those who aren't exist in our world a little differently . . .

Now that I've cleared that up, let us continue with our story.

The three moonchildren and their *jinn* went in search of Alhitan in order to defeat a monstrous stormbird wreaking

havoc upon the Sahar Peninsula. It crushed ships like they were nothing but wooden figurines, ate away at the land by the sea, and forced the people who lived there to hide in their homes to escape.

Where did it come from? you ask next.

Well, I'll tell you.

But think carefully. I'll only answer three of your questions, and you have just one left.

The stormbird was born from the rage, grief, hatred and sadness in the world. All of the emotions hidden by every person in every place for all of time. Emotions locked away for a thousand years, now released into the world.

Is your last question: *Will it come back?* If not, it should be.

Though I'm sure you'll be pleased to hear that the answer is no. The three Moonchildren and their *jinn* banished the stormbird inside eight bottles made of brass. And those same bottles now lie at the horizon, unreachable.

But emotions are fickle things, and they have a way of

creeping up on us when we least expect them. I can't promise that the danger is over just yet. In fact, it has only just begun.

I shall say no more of the stormbird, because that was Amira's story, and that isn't the story I have planned to tell you.

I am here now to tell Farah's story. Farah, who left home and was forced into no fewer than *three* accidental adventures in her twelve years of life. Farah, who has a small lizard *jinni*. Farah, who is curious to a fault . . .

It's her curiosity that drives this story, just as Amira's anger drove hers. But you'll find out more about that soon enough.

We all have stories, you see. The person whose path you crossed as you walked down the road; your relatives, who may be older than you but not necessarily wiser. And, most importantly, you. You have your own story, your own adventure.

You might know it already, or you might not. You might be able to fill the pages of this book with it, or just a

paragraph. Don't fear. You have a lifetime to find your story.

And when you do, I can't wait to hear it.

Our story starts in the middle of a very hot and barren desert. You may wonder what could happen in a place so void of life.

But plenty can happen just over our shoulders, or under our noses. It happens when we forget to pay attention, and it disappears just as we remember.

But enough chatter. I have digressed too much.

Shall we begin Farah's story?

Chapter 1

Amira sprinted through the darkness, her heart thud, thud, thudding like drums in her chest. Her throat was searing with pain as she desperately gulped down enough air to propel herself forward. Sand crunched beneath her feet, and only the sounds of her and Farah's breathing could be heard in the otherwise silent desert. That and the terrifying, hissing noise coming from the creature stalking them in the dark.

Amira peered over her shoulder while still running and stumbled, grabbing hold of Farah to steady her. The creature was faster, gaining on them, rearing up. And, quick as lightning, it –

Chapter 2

'I'm going to have to stop you there, Amira,' said Farah. 'We agreed this is *my* story to tell, not yours. And I'm going to tell it *my* way. You left out all the details. They don't even know what the creature is, what it does, or how it nearly ki—'

'I was getting to that,' Amira snapped. 'When you tell a story you need *suspense*. You need to keep the listener guessing. *You* always get straight to the point and then the rest of the story is really boring because everyone already knows what happens at the end.'

'So?' said Farah, trying not to sound offended. Layla, her lizard *jinni*, crawled from beneath Farah's nest of hair and stuck her forked tongue out at Amira. 'What's wrong with that?'

'Well,' Amira explained, 'now that you've interrupted me, they know we survived. So it's no use saying we were nearly killed because they know, now, that we weren't.'

Farah and Amira were sitting together round a pitiful fire, with nothing but sand surrounding them for miles. Amira's cat *jinni*, Namur, was resting on her lap, grumbling every so often, his tail swishing left and right. He had been invisible just moments ago, as *jinn* are in their pure form, appearing only when Amira felt the first prickle of annoyance at being interrupted.

Farah rolled her eyes. 'That's silly. Everyone knows we survived, otherwise who would be telling this story?'

'If you had just let me tell the beginning for you, everyone might have thought you were in grave danger, which would be very exciting. Then, *after* I introduced you, you could've taken over,' Amira said, her eyes flashing.

'What?' Farah tried to keep up with Amira's logic. 'You've made this all *far* too confusing.'

'No, I haven't,' insisted Amira.

Farah and Amira had taken to bickering a lot on their travels. It was the way of their friendship. Farah couldn't help noticing how Amira treated her in comparison to Leo, the third Moonchild. She was softer with him, somehow. Leo had sacrificed himself to trap the stormbird all those months ago, flying with it to the horizon. Amira was certain he was still out there, and that he would return, but Farah wasn't so sure.

Since Leo had disappeared, Amira had spent most of her time staring at the horizon. Then, one day, the sky had begun to change, and the pair had found themselves thrust into the adventure they were on today.

'Yes, you have,' snapped Farah impatiently. 'Now YOU listen . . .'

To Farah's surprise, Amira fell silent. But Farah didn't have time to celebrate the small victory, because she soon discovered it wasn't her persuasive techniques but something else entirely that had drawn Amira's attention.

Something sounded from behind them, dragging along the sand. As it inched closer, crunching against the helpless bodies of desert bugs, the fear that had immediately bloomed in Farah's chest spread round her body like roots, gripping firm. She felt both numb and alert, like a lone rabbit within a predator's reach.

'It's back,' said Farah, standing up at once and grabbing her things. Amira did the same. It was clear this wasn't the first time they had been forced to leave in a rush. Within seconds they were ready to go, their *jinn* waiting for instruction. 'Run.'

Chapter 3

Farah knew the desert well. She had grown up on its outskirts, after all. She knew the feeling of sand underfoot, the heat of the sun that scorched from above, and the freezing temperatures at night that made it feel as if you were plunged into a different world entirely.

But most of all, Farah knew about the creatures that lived in the desert, good and bad. Stories whispered in the dark as she and her cousins shared a giant bed in a cramped room. She'd heard tales of Shadhavar, with its forty-two-branched horn that played either joyful or mournful music depending on the direction of the wind; of ghouls, who whispered your worst fears before devouring your soul and consuming your flesh. And now Farah had begun weaving her own tale of the creature stalking them in the dark.

The desert was mostly her friend. But like any serious friendships, they had their ups and downs. And tonight, it was mad at her.

Farah and Amira ran blindly through the open, their bags banging against their legs, their *jinn* trailing behind. In the darkness, with nothing to break up the horizon, everything ahead was sky. Thousands of stars shone down on them, clustering around the great crescent moon watching over them as they dodged shrubs that poked out of the sand to trip them, and dunes that threatened to drag them down, their feet sinking with each step.

Something was reaching for Farah, snapping at her ankles. A large snake with a bright green body that resembled her embroidered tunic. It was diving in and out of the sand, as if swimming through it, its body glowing silver in the moonlight.

'Why is it following us?' Farah had asked after being chased the last time.

Amira shrugged. 'Food?' She'd said it casually, but Farah had seen how her hands shook and her voice broke.

But it disappears at sunrise . . . Farah mused as she ran now, trying to piece together everything that had happened since they'd entered the desert. She knew some animals slept during the day and hunted at night, but this seemed more than that. Like magic was at play.

Ever since they'd released Alhitan from its brassy prison, the nights had grown longer. Slowly. Now they began to creep into the days, threatening to swallow up the sun entirely. In the sun's absence, the world had grown cold, and Farah knew that if it continued, crops would die, people would starve, and life would cease. All because the Moonchildren hadn't realized one thing: moon magic cannot exist alone. It requires balance.

Namur sprinted ahead of Amira and Farah, as usual, the glow from his body their guiding light. But where they were going, they couldn't be sure. The creature chased them through the long nights, until they collapsed, exhausted, at dawn, and it retreated back into the shadows.

Amira began to slow now. Long, sleepless nights and dwindling resources were beginning to take their toll. Farah understood. Amira was a sea witch. And though the sea was even greater in expanse than the desert, Amira's world on her dhow, *Tigerheart*, was small. She was used to climbing to the viewing port, and sweeping the deck; she could abseil down the side of the boat, and hold the dhow's wheel for as long as she needed. But Amira wasn't used to running. Not like Farah.

Farah had been running her whole life. As a child she ran from the boys in her village who tormented her because of Layla. And, when she grew older, she ran from the officials who wanted to snatch her *jinni* away.

Now Farah was running to a place she had only heard about in stories. And she was determined to restore the balance in their world, to control the moon magic that had sat dormant for a thousand years before the *jinn* were released from their bottles.

Emotions had been freed, like caged birds. Now they threatened to take over. Like all magic, emotions had to be channelled in the right way: anger as passion, nerves as logical deduction, curiosity as discovery. But for those who weren't used to feeling or expressing emotions, anger was a tidal wave; nerves froze the person who felt them; and curiosity led to dangerous choices.

Farah dragged Amira with her, sweat forming at her brow. She felt nauseated from her exertions, but her stomach was empty – filled only with water and dates. A stitch began to build in her side, but Farah pressed on.

'I can't,' Amira said, through gritted teeth, falling to

the ground, sand flying everywhere. Namur turned back, hopping on to her shoulders, chirruping anxiously.

'You have to!'

Farah attempted to pull Amira and her *jinni* up, but it was no use. The snake was circling them now, as if deciding who to attack first. Its forked tongue stuck out, dripping saliva. The closer it came, the more Farah could smell its stale scent: like food long burnt, or ashes from a fire.

And then Farah saw it, peeking up from the horizon. The sun. The one thing that had kept the creature at bay, for reasons unknown.

'Stay here!' Farah ordered Amira, her voice wobbling only a little.

'No problem,' Amira joked between long breaths. 'I'll just – wait. Farah? Farah! What are you doing?'

Farah was running towards the snake now, in an attempt to distract it. It paused, confused by her change in tack. Farah hadn't had time to plan her next move, but she decided the safest option was to sit on top of it, trapping its head so it couldn't bite her.

She turned briefly to the horizon to see the sun creeping

up steadily. 'Come on,' she said, gritting her teeth, before launching herself into the air.

The snake let out a surprised hiss as Farah landed on its back. Its scales reminded her of the date trees she'd scuttled up as a child. Layla was tucked into her hair, as always. Pinning down the snake as planned, she glanced back to make sure Amira was OK. Her friend was watching her, mouth agape, too stunned to move.

Farah wasn't afraid. Maybe she was too tired, too fed up. Maybe, for once, she wanted to take charge of her own story. Whatever the reason, Farah now clung on while the snake swished its head violently, left and right, in an attempt to knock her off.

Farah's stomach flipped as the snake's tail suddenly whacked her across the head. She toppled to the ground, winded, with Layla desperately trying to grab on to her curls. She coughed, trying to catch her breath, just as the snake reared up, unlocking its jaw, ready to bite.

Farah covered her face with her hands, bracing herself. Something warm rolled over her body, and a bright light shone through her eyelids. Was she dead? Was this how it felt to die?

But then the snake hissed again. Farah opened her eyes just in time to see it dive into the sand. The ground rumbled for a moment, then everything stilled.

The sun. It had saved her. The creature would be gone again until the moon rose once more for another long night. Farah let out a gasp of relief as Amira and Namur trotted towards her. But something was wrong.

She couldn't feel Layla.

Farah stood, her world spinning. 'Layla?' she cried, searching all around.

Her *jinni* was nowhere to be seen. Had she been taken by the snake? Devoured? Farah's eyes filled with tears, and she opened her mouth to screech her *jinni*'s name again. But then she felt something crawl up her leg at speed.

'Layla!' Farah held her *jinni* in the palm of her hand, kissing the top of her head.

'You,' said Amira, finally reaching her. 'Are crazy.' She pulled Farah in for a hug.

Farah drank in Amira's fear, which stung her throat like hot ash. She let out a shaky, hysterical laugh, and then let the tears spill. She felt as if something heavy was weighing her down, like she had swallowed a rock.

And suddenly it was too much to bear.

Just as the stormbird had done before they defeated it, recently Farah had felt as if she was carrying the emotions of the world. She could smell them, see them; she could *feel* them too, as if they were her own. It had become worse as the nights had lengthened, though Amira didn't seem to have the same problem. Farah understood now why the stormbird had raged so much, why it had attacked. Sometimes she wanted to do the same. But instead she just cried, as she was doing now.

'Let's sleep,' Amira said gently. 'Like my mother Jamila always says: all great adventures begin with a nap.'

Farah tried to smile, but her eyelids were already drooping. The adrenaline that had pumped through her body had disappeared as quickly as the snake. As she drifted off to sleep, she thought of magic, and how it was not a gift at all, the way Amira and her sea-witch mothers believed it to be.

It was a curse.

ONE WEEK EARLIER

Chapter 4

'Just because we go on adventures doesn't mean we have to wear boring clothes,' Amira said, as she and Farah stood in front of a mirror in her cabin.

Farah peered at their reflections and frowned.

Amira was wearing a purple top with polka dots and golden flames at her cuffs. She had midnight-blue trousers speckled with stars, and a piece of golden string tied into a bow for a belt.

Farah's top and trousers were beige and ripping at the seams. In her defence, she had left home in a hurry. An official from her town had threatened to take her *jinni* Layla away and destroy her. The outfit she'd worn to flee into the night hadn't exactly been at the forefront of her mind.

Tigerheart, Amira's dhow, was sailing back to Failaka port. Amira's mothers had 'unfinished business' to attend to. It had sounded intriguing, but after some prying,

Farah and Amira discovered that even sea witches had to fill out paperwork to moor boats and make money on land.

After that, the pair decided they wouldn't bother themselves with dull adult problems any longer, and focused instead on the adventures they would go on once they arrived at Failaka. They planned to visit the souk, climb the cliffs, and get lost in the labyrinthine alleyways. And after that, Farah would return home. It was what Amira had promised when they'd first returned to *Tigerheart*.

Amira gasped now, clasping her hands to her mouth dramatically as she inspected Farah's outfit. 'You don't even have any pockets. Where in *Sahar* do you put everything?'

'I travel light,' said Farah, shrugging. But when Amira locked her in a staring competition that made Farah a little uncomfortable, she sighed and rolled her eyes. '*Fine*. You can dress me. But you're *not* getting rid of my hair nest.'

Amira squealed, clapping her hands in delight as she dived into the messy pile of clothes.

Five minutes later Farah was wearing an emerald-green tunic with tear drop sequins that shimmered in the light. It hung loosely, and Amira paired it with mint-green trousers embroidered with vertical gold stripes. They were baggy, wide set, with plenty of room to move freely.

This time, when Farah peered at their reflections, she smiled.

'You look wonderful,' said Amira proudly. 'If I say so myself. *And* you match my ring!' She held out the emerald ring she had kept from her father when they'd freed Alhitan from its brass curse.

'Where did you get these clothes from?' Farah asked, twisting round to inspect herself. The outfit was pretty, but also light. Exactly what she needed to set foot on land again.

'My mums always buy new materials at the souks we visit,' explained Amira. 'We make our own clothes out of them to suit our needs.'

'But these patterns look like they're meant for fine dresses,' said Farah, studying the embroidery.

Amira grinned. 'They are. We like to put our own twist on them. There's a pouch on the underside of your top, so you can carry things safely.'

Farah flipped up her top to find a zip pouch the exact dimensions of a book. 'Genius!'

'Now you just need to do the test,' said Amira.

'What's the test?'

'You lunge!' Amira put her hands on either side of her waist, and took a long step forward, followed by another. Her cabin was so small that it took only two lunges to get across it. 'See? Plenty of room to move.'

Farah put her hands on her waist, copying Amira's movements, and lunged once, before losing her balance and falling in a heap.

Amira giggled.

'Did I pass the test?' Farah asked.

'Perfectly.'

It was while Amira and Farah were tidying clothes away that they heard it. A crack outside, like thunder. They rushed over to Amira's cabin window. It was covered in frost, which had coated the dhow during one of the long nights. But the frost was melting as the sun began to rise again, if only briefly. Outside the sky was orange-pink, like a bruise, and lightning lit up the horizon like cracks in an eggshell.

'Do you see that?' Amira squealed, pointing so enthusiastically she elbowed Farah in the face. There wasn't much room in the cabin.

'Ow!' said Farah, rubbing her cheek as she followed Amira's line of sight. 'See what? The sun?'

'No,' answered Amira impatiently. 'Beyond the clouds.'

The clouds parted, like a gaping wound, and a strange formation of light moved in waves, like birds in flight. Farah could have sworn she saw the light take the shape of different animals. Was that a dog? No, a fox. But it transformed too quickly for her to be sure.

'What do you think it is?' asked Farah, as she watched the formations dance across the sky.

'I don't know,' admitted Amira. 'Do you think it's got something to do with the sun disappearing?'

'Maybe. At least it's getting warmer outside,' said Farah, her breath fogging up the window. Frost had never been seen before in the Sahar Peninsula, and she had found the shift alarming. What was making the nights grow longer? And could they stop it?

'For now,' answered Amira darkly. 'Who knows how

long the sun will last this time?'

She left the question hanging. They both knew something bigger was at play. Ever since they had freed the *jinn* from their bottles, defeated the stormbird and released moon magic into the world, things had changed. The nights had grown longer and the days shorter. Slowly the night spanned twelve hours, then twenty-four, and people began to question if the sun would return at all. Very quickly, sight of the sun became a cause for celebration. People would go outside again, warm their skin, unused to the frost covering their usually hot land.

'We need to fix this,' Farah finally said.

And that's how Farah found herself on her fourth accidental adventure.

Chapter 5

'But *how* do we fix this?' Amira had asked later that same day, on the dhow. 'How do we make the sun come back for good?'

Farah frowned. 'How did you know where to find Namur before?' They needed a starting point, something to get their mission going.

The pair had moved to Amira's bed, collapsing on to a pile of cushions. Namur was buried somewhere beneath them, cosy and warm, while Layla scuttled around the walls, presumably in search of bugs to devour.

Amira paused for a moment. 'It started off with a story my mothers told me, about the brass island.'

'But, when they told you the story, you didn't know *where* it was?'

Amira shook her head. 'Not until after we visited the midnight souk.'

Farah thought back to the midnight souk, and the

strange magic that lingered there. She thought back to when she had first met Amira and Leo: two other Moonchildren just like her. And she remembered the moment they had discovered the brass island, Alhitan, sitting on the back of an enormous whale. 'Not all stories are whole,' she muttered, frowning. 'Some have different parts to them, like sides of a coin.'

'What do you mean?' asked Amira.

And that's when Farah thought back. 'My teta used to tell me a story about the moon and the sun. I thought she had made it up . . .' Like Amira, Farah was raised on stories, though not to her parents' knowledge. They were buried away, like lost treasure, and Farah kept them safe, so safe that she was beginning to forget them.

'. . . But now, after everything, I'm not so sure . . .'

Amira sniffed impatiently. 'Will you stop speaking in riddles? You sound like a philosopher.'

'Sorry,' said Farah, gathering her thoughts. Her mind was like the trunk of a tree, branching off in different directions, yet tangling together. Sometimes it was hard to untangle it. 'Every night, from the age of ten, Teta Nourah told me a story, promising to finish on the thousand and first night. We didn't quite get that far.'

'And this story will help us know how to fix whatever is going on out there?' said Amira, indicating at the sky outside.

Farah nodded again.

'Well,' said Amira, bouncing up and down on her knees. 'Don't be shy. Tell your story!'

Realizing she would finally have to reveal the truth about her family, and their views on magic (something she had been holding back from Amira since they first met at the midnight souk), Farah dived into her story head first, not allowing herself to turn back.

The Tale of the Moonchild's Curse

Some time ago, a Moonchild lived in the uppermost room of a large home. The home belonged to the Moonchild's parents, and it was beautiful, straight out of a fairy tale. There were winding staircases, hidden passages, and a courtyard that surrounded the house, filled with date trees and ivy.

The Moonchild's parents were the town advisors, and they had a reputation to uphold. They threw parties and dinners, and in return they were showered with gifts and praise. All was well.

Apart from one thing.

On starting school, the Moonchild and her *jinni* had begun to garner interest. The locals whispered of a curse that followed her, bringing bad luck to anyone who crossed her. The Moonchild's parents were afraid of the curse, and so they sought counsel from a friend. That same friend told them three things, and promised that if they heeded his words, all would be well again.

Keep the Moonchild hidden away, and make it difficult for the *jinni* to reach her.

Don't let her near others, lest she infect them with her curse.

Don't encourage her magic. Talk her out of it, where possible.

Years later, and despite her parents' efforts, the Moonchild's curse still lingered. And so she kept herself away from everyone, so as not to pass it on.

Every night, after her parents were asleep, the Moonchild would sneak outside and play in the sand. With her *jinni* on her head, she climbed down her window and plunged herself into the desert. Together they hunted for bugs, dug great cavernous holes as if searching for treasure, and pretended they were sailing the seas. Night was the Moonchild's favourite time. It was when no one was around to fear her; it was when she could be herself.

While they laughed and played, the Moonchild

wondered: were there others like her? Were they cursed, too?

One night, when she had just turned twelve, the Moonchild could hear her parents laughing downstairs while she hid away in her room. There was music, and chattering; the swish of dresses, and the clop of shoes. Smoke spiralled upwards, carrying with it a perfumed haze. The Moonchild imagined what it would be like to mingle, to join in with everyone's laughter, to be normal.

Then came a familiar knocking on the Moonchild's bedroom door.

'Come in, Teta,' she said, knowing it was her grandmother immediately by her tread, and the way her jewellery jangled on the other side of the door.

Teta peered around the door with a grin on her face. She was short and frail, but each of her steps were sure. She was the sort of person who knew herself and didn't care what others thought. Unlike the Moonchild, who was always wondering if people found her annoying, or strange.

'I brought you some food,' Teta said. 'Your favourite: majboos.'

The smell of chicken and spiced rice filled the Moonchild's room, bringing with it the comfort of her grandmother's hug. The Moonchild had avoided her parents all morning while they prepared for the party that night, and she hadn't managed to make herself any food. She accepted the plate gratefully and began eating right away.

'How's Dalal?' she asked, between bites. She always worried for her younger sister, but it was difficult because her parents wanted them to stay apart. Dalal wasn't cursed, like the Moonchild, and so they still had hope for her.

Teta smiled. 'You know Dalal. She's lively, *loud*. She's playing with your cousins. They're all pretending to have a *jinni*, like you.'

The Moonchild's eyes widened. 'Baba won't be happy about that!'

Teta snorted. 'My son isn't happy about anything,' she said, a hint of bitterness to her voice. 'Let the children play. Let them learn that magic is a gift.'

'You really think it is?' The Moonchild said, hopeful. 'A gift?' She was so used to being told she was cursed.

'Of course I do!' Teta said with certainty. 'If we channel it for good, not bad.'

The Moonchild nodded. That made sense. But how could she know if *she* was good or bad? Was it her actions that determined this, or the magic that ran through her veins?

'Do you know anything else about magic?' the Moonchild asked.

'Lots and lots,' said Teta, with a glint in her eye. 'Let's eat together, and I'll tell you stories until these wretched people leave.'

The Moonchild laughed. Teta was the only person – besides Dalal – who seemed to understand her. She didn't like the flashy lifestyle her parents sought, with their big house and even bigger group of friends who wanted nothing but money and power. She cared about stories, and love, and sharing food.

'Layla,' Teta called, like a commander gathering their troops. Layla, the Moonchild's *jinni*, rustled from inside the Moonchild's nest of hair. They had been so used to hiding her that Layla had grown as tentative as her human. 'Don't think I've forgotten you,' Teta said, and she pulled out a box of insects for the lizard to devour.

'Ewwww!' said the Moonchild, almost throwing her plate of food everywhere.

Teta chuckled. 'I'm sorry, habibti, but you're going to have to get used to it. What else do you think she'll eat when you're both out in the world, exploring lives of your own?'

'You really think we'll do that?' asked the Moonchild. She didn't think she would be much good at exploring.

'Of course! Now, are you ready for the story? It's a special one . . .'

The Moonchild nodded, and settled in bed, closing her eyes. And she felt at peace, shutting the rest of the world out, as her grandmother's words wrapped around her like a blanket.

The Tale of the Sun and the Moon

At the dawn of time, before humans, and *jinn* and other creatures were born into the world, there was the Sun, and the Moon.

The Sun and the Moon did not get along. For centuries they fought for ownership, plunging the world into years of darkness, followed by years of light. In that time, the world began to die. Years of darkness meant plants didn't grow, and years of light meant rivers dried up and worse.

In order to save the world they were responsible for, the Sun and Moon reached an agreement. They would each share half the day. The Sun would rise every morning and set every evening. Only when she was gone would the Moon show her face.

The Sun was logical, preferring certainties; the Moon was emotional, preferring feeling. Together, they were the perfect balance.

After decades of working together, watching over the people of the world, the Sun fell in love with the Moon. She courted her for years, gifting her the sea and its mysteries. In turn, the Moon gave the Sun the desert.

And with them ruling as one, the world thrived. Plants grew, rivers flowed, and the creatures of the world lived long lives. And through their connection, magic was born.

The Moon chose to keep her magic hidden. She kept her children close, their location secret. She feared for them, and what might happen if their magic was found. The Sun liked to show off, liked to dazzle and sparkle, and so she made it known where her children lived: in a city that appeared where the sun shone hottest in the Sahar Peninsula.

And so, coming together in harmony, they funnelled their magic into their children, and watched over the world. And their magic grew and thrived for a millennia.

Chapter 6

Back on the dhow, Amira held Leo's old notebook in her hands – the one he had used to figure out the mystery of the stormbird. She had been scribbling the whole time Farah was speaking. Now she looked up at Farah in concern.

'Your parents tried to get rid of your magic?' she asked, her voice soft.

They were huddled in her cabin again, whispering, so Amira's mothers couldn't hear them. By the time Farah had finished telling Amira all about her past, the sun had set once more, having risen only for a few hours. The words stuck in Farah's throat, so she simply nodded.

Amira shook her head. 'How could they? What about your grandmother and sister?'

Farah sighed, blinking fiercely. 'I . . .' she began. 'I don't want to . . .'

'You don't have to talk about it,' Amira said quickly,

steering the conversation to clearer waters. 'So, if your grandmother's story is true, that means we just need to find where the sun shines hottest. If we had to visit Alhitan to free moon magic, that must mean sun magic is trapped out there, somewhere. We just need to release it to restore the balance!'

'Except for one thing,' Farah said, her heart sinking. 'How do we find the hottest part of the desert?'

'I haven't shown you my map, have I?' Amira said, wide-eyed.

Farah shook her head. 'But I don't see how a map will help. You have to know what you want your destination to be, don't you? Maps only chart your route.'

Amira rolled her eyes. 'This isn't a *normal* map. You're living with sea witches, remember?'

Amira waltzed out of her cabin to retrieve the map, and Farah was left alone with her thoughts. This was never a good thing. They always tumbled out of her head at once, muddling her mind. It was like placing your hand into a still pond, and shaking it around, stirring up dust and pebbles, obscuring your view. The truth was, Farah was jealous of Amira's life: the way she lived with her *jinni* so openly. Farah was used to hiding who she was, feeling ashamed.

Amira returned with a wooden box the size of a book, neatly painted with the sun and moon. Tucked beneath her arm was a rolled-up map. She closed her door with a slam.

'Why are you angry?' asked Farah, seeing the fire in Amira's eyes. She tried her best not to drink it in, lest it take over her body. It was like swallowing a tonic, seeping through your bones right to your fingertips.

'I thought we had agreed not to spy on each other's emotions?' Amira said through gritted teeth.

'I know,' said Farah. 'But it's always obvious when you're angry, even without Namur's appearance.'

Amira sighed and pursed her lips. 'It's just . . .'

'What's wrong?' Farah was worried now. Had something happened to one of Amira's mothers? Or was she thinking about Leo again?

'The chickens!' Amira finally said, plopping herself on to her bed with a huff.

Farah paused. 'The . . . chickens?'

'Yes!' said Amira, throwing her arms out dramatically.

'They've ruined my favourite sequinned shoes. *Again.*'

Farah couldn't help herself. She laughed.

'It's not *funny*,' insisted Amira. 'Do you know how hard it is to make sequinned shoes that are *also* practical? I swear this is revenge.'

Farah laughed louder at that, causing Layla to pause from her excursion around the room to check on her human. Namur looked at her, scandalized, from where he was trying to rest on the bed.

'Shhh!' said Amira. 'My mothers are asleep.'

Farah stopped. 'Revenge for what?' she whispered, grinning.

'Well,' said Amira, clearing her bed to make space for the map. 'They were being *really* annoying the other day. And they wouldn't stop clucking while I was trying to sleep, so Namur might have . . .'

'Might have what?'

'It wasn't *bad*,' insisted Amira, glancing at her *jinni* who was now curled up on her pillow, looking as gentle as a kitten. 'He just . . . chased them around for a bit. *Maybe* he stuck one of their heads in his mouth. I can neither confirm nor deny it.'

Farah shook her head, her mood restored. 'Let's look at this map, then.'

It took Amira a few more moments to stop sulking over her slippers before the lure of adventure pulled her back. She unfurled the map, laid it flat on her bed, and lit the single candle she kept by her bedside. Namur hopped down from his resting place and huddled into a corner, in a huff.

'It's a little dark,' Farah teased as Amira pulled down her blinds.

'It's *supposed* to be dark,' snapped Amira, pulling the lid of the box open. Inside the lid was a clockface, but instead of numbers it held symbols of the moon, stars and sun, with three hands rather than two.

An illumination sprouted from the box, surrounding the cabin. It was the night sky, just as it looked outside: the moon shining down and the stars twinkling. And Farah and Amira were standing amongst it, like giants. Farah waved her hand over the stars, watching in fascination as she moved through them like a ghost.

'It's just a projection,' Amira explained as Layla crawled out of Farah's hair for a better look. 'Watch this. When I move this hand, it turns back time so we can watch the sun from a few moments ago. That's how I found the midnight souk, by putting the hand forward to see when the blood moon would appear.'

'Wow,' said Farah, leaning forward. 'Did you make this?'

Amira shook her head. 'My mothers have had it for years. They found it at a souk.'

'How will you know where the hottest point is?'

'By inspecting the map,' explained Amira. She turned the biggest hand back, and night turned to day. The room was filled with sunshine, and the odd cloud floating around Farah's shoulders.

Amira played around for a bit, tongue sticking out of her mouth, until she was satisfied. 'There, that's when the sun shines hottest.'

'What now?' asked Farah.

'Now we see where the sunbeam lands.'

'There!' said Farah, pointing at a ray of sun that shone on one particular point of the map.

Amira checked the hand of the clock again to make sure it was properly positioned. 'Hold the map steady,' she instructed. 'So we're sure we have the right place.'

They checked three times just to be certain. The midday sun beamed down somewhere north of Failaka. Amira explained it would change a little, because the earth tilted slightly every day. And the nights growing longer and days shorter might add another complication. But she assured Farah they would keep checking it and adjusting their route as they went along.

'It's what every good navigator does,' Amira said, before frowning. 'You know, I've never been that far inland before.'

'I have,' said Farah pursing her lips. She had realized, now, where the sun had fallen.

Into the middle of a desert.

The very same desert she escaped to when she had left home.

Chapter 7

'Be *quiet*,' Amira whispered fiercely, after Farah had dropped their pack on the floor for the second time.

Farah was usually so good at creeping around, but tonight she was nervous. Perhaps because she knew she was heading in the direction of home. The two Moonchildren were standing in the main cabin, ready to leave Failaka and begin their new adventure to find and free the source of sun magic to restore balance to the world. They hoped that doing so would bring the sun back, and stop the nights from growing even longer. All they had to go by was a single mark on a map. But didn't all great discoveries start small?

The days leading up to their departure were tricky for Farah. The closer they got to Failaka and the crowds of people on land, the more she struggled with everyone's emotions. Amira could smell them and see them too, but with Farah it was different. Fear seeped down her throat, choking her; sadness weighed her down. Even the emotions that were usually sweet were difficult to stomach. Joy was like eating too much cake, sugar coating your lips and giving you a bellyache. After a while, Farah could barely move.

'Why don't you try one of my new tonics?' Jamila suggested when she could see Farah struggling. 'To help you understand your feelings?'

Amira's mother assumed that whatever was bothering Farah was an ailment of the heart. And in some ways, she wasn't wrong. But how could Farah possibly understand her own feelings when she was so full of everyone else's? Everyone's worries were her own; her joy was dependent on them too. It was why she was so curious. She wanted to soak in the world around her, and understand the people in it. But somewhere, along the way, she had lost herself.

'How does it work?' asked Farah, studying the bottle in Jamila's hand.

The tonic was clear. Jamila explained that Farah needed to add an essence of herself to make it work. The best way to find that essence was to use Amira's powers. Everyone had a smell that followed them, hidden beneath each layer of emotion. Leo's was orange, Amira's was wood. But Amira couldn't seem to find Farah's.

'It changes too much,' Amira explained. 'I can't break through the layers to sense the source.'

And so Farah never got to try the tonic, because she was too busy changing like the winds to suit everyone around her.

Amira's mothers were asleep when Amira and Farah snuck out. In the corner, Ramady the goat rested with her kids. One of them woke, squinting at the Moonchildren and their *jinn* before wagging its tail and running over.

'Not now, Hamra,' Amira said, carrying her back to bed. 'You'll wake my mamas.'

Hamra was holding something in her mouth. A slipper. The one Amira had been upset over.

'It was *you*!' Amira said, horrified. 'Not the chickens at all!'

'You know,' whispered Farah, taking the slipper from Amira and inspecting it, 'it doesn't look like a chicken *or*

a goat did this. It looks more like a mouse, see?' She showed Amira the markings.

'That's impossible,' Amira dismissed. 'Namur would never allow a mouse on the dhow!'

'Shh! You're making the most noise of all of us,' Farah whispered.

Amira scowled at her, before placing the note she had written to her mothers on the table. All the while, Farah couldn't help the nagging feeling that she was right. It was a mouse. She recognized the markings well from childhood. A mouse had snuck into her home once and chewed at her curtains. Somehow it had become Farah's fault, and so, like all her bad memories, it was etched in her mind.

But Amira was right about one thing: Namur wouldn't let a mouse live on the dhow. So why was this mouse allowed aboard?

The pair and their *jinn* left *Tigerheart* with a bakhoor

pot, some dates and water, Leo's gloves and notebook, and Amira's magical map.

Farah had never been to Failaka. And so, beneath the full moon, Amira gave her a tour. She showed her the port master's house, restored from when the stormbird had dragged it to the seas. And, after a last goodbye to the ocean, the pair walked through the alleyways towards the souk. It stood empty now, pieces of discarded cloth and miscellanea left behind.

While Amira guided them, Farah couldn't help thinking that it was her friend telling their story, not her.

It was sunrise when they crossed into the desert, the second they had seen since spotting the light formations out at sea. If all went well, they would each return home within the week.

But of all the preparations Farah and Amira had made, and everything they had considered before setting off on their adventure, they missed one very crucial point. The desert writes its own story, and the stories of all those who journey across it.

And Farah and Amira's stories were no longer in their hands.

IN THE DESERT

Chapter 8

Farah woke first. She had barely slept, drifting in and out of dreams of her family, and the decisions she and Amira had made on the dhow. They had mapped their journey so carefully, but already their plans were fraying at the seams, like Farah's old clothes.

The sun was beginning to set, giving way to another long night. Farah took advantage of the heat, basking in the sun, letting it warm her skin while it could. How long had it been up? A few hours? And how long would the moon visit this time, bringing with it darkness and cold?

It was eerily quiet in the desert. Amira was sound asleep, and Farah's worries wormed their way into her mind, with nothing else to distract her. Was Teta's story real? Was there really a city out here? Or had Farah led them into unnecessary danger?

A hollow feeling formed in the pit of her stomach as

she thought of her younger sister Dalal, and how the changes in the world were affecting her. Farah and Dalal had been close growing up. They would share a bed, even though they each had their own room, and would play games and whisper their deepest thoughts until morning crept up on them. As they grew up and Farah's powers strengthened, Farah's parents kept them apart. They feared their daughter's magic, as if they were worried she would pass it along, like an illness, to her sister.

Farah shook the thoughts aside and buried them, the way she buried their dying campfire each morning in the sand.

They were quickly running out of food. The long nights and the snake they spawned had slowed Amira and Farah's progress, and it seemed they weren't any closer to finding the city. Farah didn't want to admit it, but she feared that they might not make it out alive. She sighed, sitting up and untangling her hair as best she could. If she couldn't sleep, she may as well get up properly.

A bird glided overhead, its shadow throwing shapes on to the sand. It let out a cry, and then it dived, presumably to catch its prey. It must just be waking up for the day,

Farah thought, hoping it would find its fill.

The desert was different to the sea. The horizon didn't fade from sky to sea in a rainbow of blue with possibilities hidden in between. It was sharp. There was no mistaking it.

Or so Farah thought.

Today she could see something else in the distance. A building the colour of sand, surrounded by date trees: a burst of life amid the haze of the desert. From here, it looked small enough for Farah to cup it in the palm of her hand. But it was unmistakable, nonetheless.

The building was surrounded by a haze of sand, and it looked like a mirage.

Farah blinked, and rubbed her eyes, to check they weren't playing tricks on her. Then, when she found the building was still there, she shook Amira awake.

'Amira!' Farah had planned not to disturb her friend, but this was the first sign of life they had seen in days. 'Amira, wake up!'

Just at that moment, the sun set fully, and the colour faded from the sky. Amira whacked Farah around the head in an attempt to push her away.

'Leave me alone,' she grumbled, still half asleep.

Namur, who had previously been invisible, slowly began to appear with Amira's anger. He woke, stretching out from beneath a blanket they had all shared, paws pointed like a ballerina's toes. He peered up at Farah curiously.

'Namur,' Farah said, deciding the *jinni* was a better bet. She pointed into the distance. 'Look.'

The *jinni* followed her line of sight, turned back at Farah, and yawned, his sharp teeth glinting in the light. Then he tucked himself up against Amira once more.

Farah sighed. 'Layla?'

The lizard *jinni* seemed to know what Farah was asking. She crawled out from Farah's nest of hair on to her shoulders, and scrambled down her body, looping round and round her legs to the ground. Then she scuttled beneath the blanket where Amira and Namur were sleeping.

Farah counted down. *Three, two, o–*

'Ahhhh! The snake, it's got me!' Amira screamed, jumping up and gripping Farah's shoulders. But she stopped, frowning. 'What are you laughing about?'

'It's just Layla.' Farah giggled as her *jinni* returned to her hair.

Amira fell silent, her eyes like daggers. Then she took a deep breath. 'Farah!' she yelled. 'I can't believe you did that! You're so –'

Farah was now used to Amira's outbursts. She simply turned Amira's body so it was facing the speck in the distance. 'See?'

'What am I looking at?' said Amira dully. 'I see nothing.'

Farah peered past Amira to the building in the distance, only to see that it wasn't there now. All that was left was a cloud of dust.

'Oh . . .' she said, her heart dropping. She had hoped they had found their first glimpse of the city, that they might be safe soon. Had she been mistaken? Was it just a mirage after all? Something told her it wasn't. She was determined to watch out for it until she had answers.

'Well?' said Amira, yawning.

'Nothing,' Farah muttered. 'Go back to sleep.'

Chapter 9

Farah, Amira and their *jinn* trudged through the desert in the dark, flinching every time any sound that resembled the snake's movements met their ears. A thousand stars shone above them, the horizon blending into the sky in an inky haze. The moon watched over her children, never leaving their side.

The temperatures slowly dropped until Farah could see her breath fog in front of her. She and Amira stopped speaking, to preserve their energy. As the hours stretched ahead, they walked, step by step, in the direction of the spot marked on the map. Eventually, with no real indication of the time, aside from their weary bodies and tired eyes, the Moonchildren and their *jinn* settled down once more for a sleepless night of monsters stalking them in the dark.

After their third walk through the next long night, which

seemed to stretch further than the last, the pair and their *jinn* settled down at their camp. While Farah put the fire together, Amira pulled out their map and turned the hands forward in time. Sunrise would arrive in just over a few hours; the map seemed to know.

How? Farah wondered. What sort of magic did it hold? Whatever it was, she was pleased. Sleeping and waking in the dark had made her drowsy, and she felt as if she would never shake off the cold that seeped into her bones.

Amira moved the hands again, readjusting until the sun was positioned at the middle of its next rise. Farah let the projection of the sun wash over her, closing her eyes and pretending for just a moment that it was real.

They had to reroute to the west, a little; not enough to throw them off track completely. Given the challenges they had faced, Farah was pleased.

But Amira didn't look very happy. 'We should be able to see it by now,' she said, peering into the distance. 'Lights, or something . . .'

'Are you sure?' said Farah, her gut clenching. Amira was gazing in the same direction as the building she had spotted earlier, though nothing was there now.

'Maybe we're still too far away?'

Amira rolled her eyes. 'I've been lookout on the dhow since I was six. I think I know when to spot land.'

'But we aren't at sea,' countered Farah. 'We're in the desert.'

'Are we?' said Amira sarcastically, peering around her in mock surprise. 'Oh my, I hadn't realized. Thanks for reminding me!'

Farah opened her mouth to speak, but she knew it was no use. She was going to tell Amira about the building she had seen earlier, but her friend had already turned her back. It was best to leave her for a few moments. Like a hot cup of tea, Amira needed time to cool down.

Still, Farah couldn't help but compare once more how much gentler Amira was when Leo was around. He had been steady, sure, like waves rolling to the shore. Amira was a fire, drawing you in, charring you and spitting you out. Farah wasn't exactly sure what *she* was, but it definitely didn't mix well with fire.

Farah was scared feeling aimless, out of control. This was meant to be *her* story, and she didn't feel in charge of it at all. When they had sailed to defeat the stormbird,

Amira seemed to know what to do. Now it was Farah's turn, and she was getting it all wrong.

It didn't help that Amira's frustration was seeping into Farah's blood, setting her chest alight. She wished she could block it out, but she didn't know how. She wished for sunlight, when she didn't feel Amira's emotions as strongly. They were still there, of course, but not as prominent.

That's when Farah noticed the pattern. If her powers faded with the sun because they came from moon magic, could the snake be connected to moon magic too, like the stormbird? Was that why it only attacked at night?

'Of course!' said Amira, when Farah voiced her suspicions. She scribbled something down in Leo's notebook, their short fight forgotten.

Farah decided it was best to keep the strange building that appeared with the sun to herself for now. She didn't want to get Amira's hopes up in case she was wrong. But next time it appeared, she was determined not to miss it.

Layla crawled out from Farah's hair, down her arm, and darted into the distance like a shooting star. She, at least, was getting her fill from hunting in the sands.

Namur was less comfortable. He draped himself across Amira's lap, completely limp. He didn't much enjoy eating dates, preferring fresh fish and chicken. And despite their circumstances, he seemed to expect the same meals he was used to receiving at sea.

'What about your teta?' asked Amira suddenly.

Farah's heart picked up pace whenever her grandmother was mentioned. 'What about her?'

'Could we send her a message? Ask her to help? She must have the answers we're looking for.'

Farah paused. Then she sighed. 'No.'

'Why?' Amira frowned.

Farah took a deep breath, and explained.

The Tale of Teta's Last Story

In the months following the party, Teta told the Moonchild stories about magic born in the skies and inside our hearts. She told the Moonchild about sea witches and creatures from the wild; about souks and mermaids, and music and love.

One night, Teta looked more tired than usual, and a little sad. She peered up at the Moonchild with watery eyes. 'I hope you remember my stories,' she said. 'Carry them with you. Cherish them.'

The Moonchild smiled, her *jinni* rustling in her hair. 'Of course!' She pulled her teta in for a long hug, taking in her scent. She could tell, then, that something was wrong. Her grandmother didn't smell like roses as usual. She smelled like something the Moonchild couldn't distinguish, but that brought visions of dying flowers into her head, and shorn trees.

'Goodnight, habibti,' Teta whispered, waving at the Moonchild from her door.

The last she saw of her grandmother was her manicured hands, nails painted emerald green.

Teta left behind her stories. The Moonchild never knew if they were real or not, but she hoped they were. They would remind her, if only for a brief moment, that she wasn't alone.

Maybe Teta was right. Maybe magic was a gift, not a curse.

But as the weeks passed, and the Moonchild was left in her room alone with her *jinni*, she began to question everything her grandmother had told her.

Some children grew up wanting adventure. Others grow up wanting to be normal. The Moonchild thought she had wanted adventure, like the stories she had been told. But she realized all she really wanted was to play with her cousins, and make friends at school, and *pretend* to go on adventures, like her sister. She wanted to read books, and draw strange creatures from the stories she read, and make fake potions. And then she wanted to retreat into the arms of her parents at night, safe and loved, instead of being shut away.

With Teta gone, the Moonchild's parents became stricter. They forbade her from seeing her sister unsupervised. Dalal knocked on her door at night and asked to play, but the Moonchild turned her away, even after her parents had long gone to bed.

The family hosted parties the Moonchild wasn't invited to, and gatherings they made excuses for her not to attend. And slowly, the Moonchild believed herself cursed again.

When the Moonchild fled into the night, her *jinni* in tow, she locked away the memories of her grandmother and the stories she had shared. Because the transformation was complete. The Moonchild was the cursed creature her parents had made her to be.

And she knew that night that she wasn't the hero of the story. She wasn't the main character at all. The Moonchild was the villain.

The one destined to lose.

Chapter 10

'That's not true,' said Amira. 'You aren't the villain.'

Farah sighed. 'Look what I did.' She spread her arms out as if trying to hold the darkness in her hands.

'What *we* did,' said Amira. 'And it wasn't our fault. We had to defeat the stormbird to stop it from destroying the Sahar Peninsula. It attacked the midnight souk and ruined people's homes. We didn't know moon magic would take over like this. What else could we have done?'

Farah wanted to disagree with Amira's points, or think of another way they could have defeated the stormbird without releasing chaos. But right now, she felt too tired and sad to think of a better solution.

'And anyway, villains aren't always the bad people in the stories,' Amira continued.

'Yes they are,' Farah replied, a little vehemently this time. 'Why else do they always have a sad ending?'

'Because,' said Amira snootily, 'they're usually the ones

who are misunderstood. Look at me. Wouldn't someone think *I* was a villain, because I'm always so angry? But I'm not. I'm the hero.' And she winked.

Farah laughed.

'So are you, when you finally learn how to tell a good story,' Amira said. She sighed. 'And sometimes good people have bad endings too . . .'

Farah knew she meant Leo, and her father, whom she had lost as they freed Alhitan. All Amira had of him now was his emerald ring, which she twisted round her finger as she spoke. Farah shuffled closer and rested her head on Amira's shoulder. Amira gripped her hand firmly.

They suddenly heard the sound of something dragging and crunching across the sand. Amira jumped, thinking it was the snake again.

'Layla!' Farah said half delighted, half disgusted. 'What in the name of Sahar . . .'

Farah's *jinni* had found the fresh carcass of something Farah did not recognize, and had somehow managed to pull it all the way to where they were camped. Namur perked up.

'It's for you,' Farah told Namur. She knew Layla would

never eat it herself.

Namur pulled himself up, purring like a kitten, and sniffed his gift. For a moment he hesitated, before taking a large bite.

As Namur ate, and Layla returned to hunt for herself, Amira pulled from her bag a small box of woodchips, taken from her home on the dhow. She pulled one out, and Farah could immediately smell it: wood, rose and orange. Amira's favourite. Amira snapped the piece of wood into pieces and placed them on top of some coal she had already prepared for her bakhoor pot. Soon the smoke took a life of its own. It swayed left and right, waiting for instruction. Farah itched to try it herself, but waited patiently for her friend.

Amira nodded at Farah, grinning. 'I'm going to tell you stories about when magic has done good.'

For the rest of the night, Amira shared her adventures out at sea with her mothers. Some tales Farah had heard; others she hadn't. It was only as Farah was getting ready to sleep that she realized the snake hadn't appeared.

'Maybe it's because we were telling stories? My mothers always say that stories hold magic,' Amira said earnestly, when Farah pointed this out. 'Did you feel it, when I spoke? Did it hum through your veins?'

Farah grinned. 'I did,' she said, and it was the truth.

Maybe, for just a moment, they were safe.

That night Farah dreamed of sand.

She had shrunk to the size of a lizard and was wading through it, slipping in and out of a sandy grave. Miniscule grains seeped into her ears, eyes and mouth. It was all she could taste and see. But still she moved, faster and faster, somehow. It was as if she was being pulled under, dragged through the sand by a force she did not recognize.

She dipped into the sand. And then out. Hoping each time it would be the last. Farah felt as if she was drowning, as if she was swimming in the ocean, the waves toppling her, pulling her under. She couldn't breathe, couldn't speak. Everything was a haze of black and white, the colour gone from her world.

Finally, Farah sank. Down down down.

And this time, she did not surface.

Farah sat up, gasping for air.

'Layla?' she called automatically. She always sought her *jinni* when she needed comfort. 'Layla?' she said again, a little louder.

Amira was fast asleep. Namur stirred from where he was curled into Amira's belly, her legs wrapped around his body. He sniffed the air once, twice, his eyes still closed, and then settled back to sleep.

'Layla,' Farah tried for a third time, her voice wobbling. Hot tears spilled down her face as she thought of the nightmare. She felt shaky, cold with fear.

Finally, from somewhere in the darkness, her lizard *jinni* slid up her arm and back into her hair. Only when Farah could feel Layla's weight, did she settle.

She woke again when the sun was setting once more. The strange building was there again, just as she had seen it before, with its date trees and the haze of sand surrounding it. This time Farah didn't take her eyes off it. She tried not to blink, for fear it would disappear. She knew about mirages, about the way our minds trick us when we are tired and hungry, and she wanted to be sure this was real.

As the last ray of light disappeared, Farah saw the building sink into the sand, surrounded by a cloud of dust. And, moments later, after the dust had settled, it was as if it had never been there at all.

Chapter 11

'I could never be a desert dweller,' Amira said the next
night, while they huddled by the fire.

It was especially cold; a deep ache seeped into Farah's
bones. Moving her joints hurt, and her breaths were
sharp, cooling her body even more. The fire wasn't
enough to warm them, and she huddled close to Amira
and Namur's soothing glow.

Things were shifting again. The life they had seen – the
odd shrub, and creeping animal – was slowly disappearing.
Farah couldn't tell whether it was because they had
wandered deeper into the desert, close to its centre now,
or whether this was the moon's doing. Were things
already beginning to die due to the lengthening nights?
Could they really restore everything by releasing sun
magic?

'You couldn't?' asked Farah, her teeth chattering.
'Why not?'

'Because when you live in the desert and move around a lot, you have to pack your things over and over. And then you have to *un*pack them too. It's so boring and tedious. Packing is my least favourite thing to do in the entire *world*,' Amira answered, waving her arms around.

Farah smiled. 'I guess you don't ever have to pack when your house moves with you.'

'Exactly,' said Amira. 'Why can't there be dhows in the desert? Why do we have to *walk* so much? Walking is the second thing I hate most.'

How well Amira knew herself! Farah thought. Her anger ruled her personality, but past the angry displays, Farah could see exactly what sort of person Amira was: passionate, kind and loyal. And Leo, though nervous, was thoughtful, and logical, and sweet.

Those things were plain to see because their emotions were so free.

But what about Farah? She wasn't even sure of her own emotions most of the time. If Amira was fire, and Leo was water, then what was she?

'What's the thing you hate most?' she asked.

'Chickens,' Amira said with certainty. 'Their poop gets

in the cracks of the wood and you have to scrape it out
with a –'

'O-K!' Farah said, interrupting with a disgusted look on
her face. 'You really *don't* have to elaborate.'

Amira cackled, clearly enjoying Farah's reaction. Then,
as she often did, she steered the conversation in a different
direction, like a dhow sailing to new lands. 'Do you want
to tell a story tonight?'

Farah thought back to her parents. They were where
her stories always seemed to lead. In the cold desert night,
with strange creatures chasing them and the very balance
of the world disrupted, it was hard not to agree with their
belief that magic was a curse.

'Farah?' said Amira, waving a hand in front of her face.

'Of course!' said Farah, pushing her worries aside.

Except they didn't move aside.

They burrowed deep inside her, ready to crawl out
when she least expected it.

Farah and Amira prepared the bakhoor pot together,
with coal and scented woodchips. This time Farah picked
her own scent: rose, for her grandmother. She hoped it
would give her strength to last the long night.

Then she heard it.

Heavy, scraping thuds.

'Layla?' Farah asked, hoping the little lizard was just dragging in a carcass like the night before. But her *jinni* had only just gone to hunt, and in any case, Farah couldn't sense her presence. 'Is Namur invisible, Amira?' she tried next, though she already knew the answer.

Amira nodded, eyes fearful. 'I think it's . . .'

'. . . the snake,' Farah finished, her mouth turning dry.

She wanted to cry. Give up. She wasn't sure how much more desert and magic she could take. Namur hissed, and Layla scuttled up Farah's arm into her hair. The stars and moon watched over them, but Farah knew they had to deal with this alone.

The snake towered up out of the sand like before, and screeched so loud it pierced through Farah's ears. It slammed down, sending a whoosh of sand over the campfire and extinguishing it. Everything went dark apart from the moon, which shone brighter than ever.

Farah gritted her teeth and turned to the bakhoor pot. The smoke gathered around her, making her eyes water. It swayed left and right, waiting for instruction. And

Farah thought of something Amira had said, about stories and their magic . . .

She leaped away from Amira, clutching the pot firmly. She could hear the snake swimming around the sand, sending waves in their direction. As loud as she could, Farah told a story, her breath fogging in the cold. And, as she did, the smoke took shape.

'Once there were two young Moonchildren and their *jinn* alone in the desert. They had travelled for days, and they were hungry and tired. To make matters worse, they were being chased by a monster, who tormented the children and scared them.'

The snake hissed and rose above Farah, covering her in shadow. The ground around her feet rumbled and shifted. Farah feared she would sink into the sand, like in her nightmares. She screamed as the snake swooped down to swallow her up, missing by inches.

'Keep going!' said Amira, her hand squeezing Farah's arm.

It was like she had broken a spell. Farah spoke quickly, hoping the smoke could keep up with her words.

'One night, when the monster approached, the Moonchildren were scared again –'

The hissing snake reared up once more. In the moonlight, Farah could see it shake its head left and right, as if it was in pain.

'– but then the second Moonchild remembered the strength of her words . . .'

Amira nodded encouragingly. Farah plunged on.

'Beneath the watch of the moon, a great horse arrived to protect the Moonchildren. It was grey-black, with a white mane, and powerful legs that carried it through the desert at top speed –'

Farah could feel it before she saw it: the power of her words. The sound of hooves clip-clopped towards them, followed by a neigh that pierced through the night.

'The horse captured the monster, snaring it, and galloped with it on its back, far, far away . . .'

Farah heard the horse's hooves pick up pace, then fade away. The snake's screech disappeared into the night. And everything fell silent.

'With the monster gone, the two Moonchildren and their *jinn* were safe once more,' she finished in wonder.

The smoke lingered, like a protective cloak, keeping them warm. And for the first time since setting foot in the desert, Farah felt like they had a chance of surviving.

Chapter 12

Farah woke to the taste of sand on her tongue. She'd had another dream where she felt as if the desert were swallowing her up, and she was powerless to it.

She had once known how to bend the sands to her will. She'd known exactly what sorts of flowers would bloom and where, and how to catch scorpions with nothing but a piece of string. Now the desert felt like a stranger – hostile and unfamiliar. It had changed. Or maybe it was Farah who was different.

It was just before sunset. Farah was ready this time, waiting. The sun had tried to evade them again, but they had readjusted their route, and followed it like loyal subjects might follow their ruler.

Farah and her sister had often climbed up to the roof of their house at sunrise, when their parents were asleep, and watched the sky, taking it in turns to count down to the moment when the sun hit the horizon.

'You have to stay home from school today!' her sister would declare when she won their competition. 'And play with me.' And they would watch Layla scuttle back from her night's hunt to meet them, inventing the adventures she'd had while they were asleep.

Unlike Namur, who turned invisible during those brief moments when Amira wasn't angry, Layla was always around because Farah was always curious. Those with curious minds will know there is seldom a moment when you aren't thinking about something: about why clouds form certain shapes, or if animals feel the same emotions as humans. Or why the city Farah and Amira were searching for seemed to have been replaced by a strange building that only appeared in the sunlight.

And Farah was glad Layla was always there. It meant she was never alone, even when everyone else had shunned her. Amira and her mothers couldn't get away from one another on the dhow. And they never seemed to want to.

A wave of guilt washed over Farah as she thought of how she had left her sister behind. But she had done it for Layla. She tried to ignore the small thought nagging at the back of her mind, that she and the other Moonchildren had made everything worse. Maybe if Farah had given up Layla, none of this would have happened . . .

That was the bad side to a curious mind. Your thoughts turned into trains that could lead to the saddest of destinations. But Farah stopped the train and took a new path.

She wiped the sleep from her eyes, hoping it might wipe her thoughts clean too. And that's when she noticed it.

Burrowing into the burnt out ashes from the fire was a mouse. It was sandy coloured, almost blending with the ground, with long legs and even longer ears.

Farah could smell it too, like burnt milk, its sweetness lingering. Farah recognized the scent from being around Dalal, but it took her some moments to place it.

Mischief.

Was this the same mouse who had chewed through Amira's shoes on the dhow? Had it followed them out here? Why? What did it want?

The mouse suddenly launched itself at her. Farah fell back to the ground. She didn't even have time to scream. It scrambled into Farah's hair.

The next thing she knew, the mouse was scuttling along the sand. Something hung from its mouth, luminescent purple-and-blue. In a second, Farah's heart sank, like a broken dhow.

It was Layla. The mouse had snatched Layla.

Now it was running towards the building that appeared at every sunrise and disappeared as the moon arrived. Farah and Amira had slept through the short days, the brief moments they were safe from the stalking snake, which is why Farah had only glimpsed it. The building was much closer now, only a short walk away.

Farah launched herself at the mouse, running quicker than she ever had before. At the last moment she dived, landing hard in the sand, sending dust everywhere. Her hand gripped something wormlike and firm. The mouse's tail.

They were just outside the building now. Farah could see the cloud of dust reaching for them, as if warning them away. But she wasn't turning back. Not without Layla.

She moved quickly, her hands reaching for the mouse's tiny jaws. She prised them open and snatched Layla back.

She was breathless, her heart clamouring. Then – pain.

The mouse had bitten her, its fangs sinking into her skin.

Farah screamed, her voice echoing across the desert. Layla scuttled back into her hair. The mouse raced away.

Farah had to know what the mouse was, why it was here, and why it had just tried to snatch Layla.

She turned back, to check on Amira and Namur at the camp. They were sleeping peacefully through all the drama unfolding around them.

From the window of the building just ahead of her now, Farah saw the mouse peer at her and Layla, as if daring them to follow. She should have turned back, should have told Amira and Namur what had happened, but something stopped her. First a snake, now a mouse. What curse was following them into the desert? And what was this mysterious building?

Farah pushed hard against the sand that whirled around her. It tried to push her back, but she was stronger, more determined. Reaching the house, she swung the door open and forced her way inside.

Darkness.

Silence.

Then . . .

A crash. The storm burst through the windows, glass flying everywhere, threatening to pull Farah and Layla up into the sky.

The storm whipped at her face and stung her skin. It pulled her to and fro. Farah slammed into the wall and sank to the floor, pain shooting up her arm and shoulder. She crawled to a corner, unable to see anything. She patted around, hoping to reach something she could hold on to. Layla clung desperately to her hair.

And then, without warning, the building collapsed.

And Farah was falling, sinking into the sand, just as she had in her nightmares.

Chapter 13

It's me, your narrator. Is that what I'm supposed to call myself? Maybe not. Amira says I don't leave room for intrigue, but this is my story, and I'll tell it how I like.

I won't tell you the end of the story this time. I'll let *you* guess what happens.

As I let my curiosity take over and followed the mouse into the building, I found myself separated from my friend, not knowing if she was safe.

If you look back at my story, you'll see I left clues along the way. But if you've ever been to the desert (have you?) you'll know clues are hard to find there, buried as they are in the sand. Still, I think it's worth a try.

Have you found them? The clues?

No?

I suppose you're wondering what happened after the sandstorm hit, and the building collapsed. I'm alive, of

course, otherwise who is telling you this story? But that isn't to say *everyone* survived.

I'll give you three possibilities.

I found myself buried in the sand, and fought my way out to find Amira. We found the city together and restored sun magic to the world.

I found myself buried in the sand, and was separated from Amira. I found the city alone, and we each went on our separate paths.

I found myself buried in the sand, and was separated from Amira. I found the city alone, and was forced to make a difficult decision.

Let's play a game. Have you heard of two lies and a truth? Two of those options are a lie, and one is the truth. It isn't the full truth, because that would be giving too much away.

Go on, guess. Which one is the truth?

I'll give you time . . .

Are you ready?

I suppose I should continue my story, and let you know which one of these fates befell me and Amira. If only she could have seen me tell *this* part of the story. She would have so enjoyed it.

But as it happens . . . Well, I'll just let you find out.

Chapter 14

Farah woke spluttering and coughing, her mouth dry. Sand crunched between her teeth, and she struggled to catch her breath.

What had just happened?

A sandstorm. Farah had been following the mouse into the building and the building had collapsed. So where was she now?

She quickly checked in her nest of hair to make sure Layla was safe. Her *jinni* licked her wounded palm in reassurance. Farah wiped the sand from her eyes with her hands. The pain of the mouse bite was returning. Her shoulder ached, and she felt more exhausted than she had during their entire journey.

She was in a tunnel. It was gloomy, and it took some time for Farah to focus. But when she eventually could, her gaze landed on a boy.

He was about Farah's age, with dark brown skin and

brass goggles on top of his head that seemed to be opaque. He was wearing a long white tunic, with dark trousers cuffed in golden thread. A gold belt wound around his waist, and he was holding what looked like a flute. He had a brown glove on one arm, and was holding that arm out as if reaching for something.

'Who are you?' said Farah, just as a falcon landed on the boy's arm. It let out a cry Farah recognized. Was it the same hunting bird she had seen in the desert?

'My name is Hamad,' the boy said. He paused, as if considering his next sentence. 'Are you hurt?' His eyes travelled to Farah's right arm, which was clutched in her left. Her shoulder throbbed, and blood coated her palm.

'I'll be fine,' said Farah quickly.

The boy raised his eyebrows. 'It doesn't look fine,' he said, approaching her slowly, like she was a lizard about to dart away at any sudden movement.

Farah's eyes travelled to the falcon – and then she knew that she could trust Hamad. The falcon had brown feathers in a tortoiseshell pattern, with a black hooked beak, and beady yellow eyes. But it was no ordinary bird. It had the same glowing skin as Layla and Namur. The same as Semek, Leo's fish. The bird was a *jinni* – one of the *jinn* they had released from Alhitan!

'Her name is Manayer,' Hamad said with a smile. 'She's my guiding light. What's yours called?'

'Layla. And I'm Farah,' Farah said, returning his smile. Holding her hand out, she asked, 'Did you see the mouse that did this?'

Hamad inspected her wound. 'It looks painful.'

'It is,' Farah said impatiently. 'Have you seen it?'

'No,' Hamad said, unfazed. 'But we need to get this cleaned up. Then we'll talk.'

Farah looked around. How could they clean the bite down in this tunnel? She had other questions too. Who was Hamad? How had he found his *jinni*? Why did he have a flute, tucked in his belt now, and goggles on his head?

She suddenly noticed a shining gate ahead of them in the tunnel. Beyond the gate, there were voices – their echoes just about reaching them.

Farah decided to ask her most pressing question first.

'Where am I?' she asked. She could tell they were underground, but she couldn't see a way out.

'It's a long story,' said Hamad, offering no further explanation.

Farah took the water pouch he handed her, sipped and gargled, spitting out the sand in her mouth. Then she drank. Her throat was sore, and it ached, but the water was soothing. She turned to Hamad and his *jinni* Manayer again. The falcon was studying her closely.

'Well?' Farah said 'Tell your story, so I can get back to my friend.'

Hamad pursed his lips. 'I'm afraid you won't be able to do that. Not for a while, at least.'

Chapter 15

'Why not?' Farah asked, crossing her arms.

Hamad's face softened, surprising her. 'The building you fell through was a gateway to this tunnel,' he explained gently. 'And it's only open when the sun is up.'

'But the sun *is* up,' Farah pointed out.

'Not any more. It set while you were in the building. We can't do anything now but wait through the next long night. And get your hand cleaned up.'

'Stop going on about my hand,' Farah snapped, channeling Amira's haughtiness. 'I have to get back up to Amira. We're searching for a city. And she's stuck out there in a sandstorm. What if –'

Hamad shook his head calmly. 'The sandstorm only surrounds the house. Your friend will be fine. And anyway, I'm taking you to the city.'

Farah narrowed her eyes suspiciously, trying not to look hopeful. 'What city?'

Hamad raised his eyebrows. 'Is this a trick question? The city you're searching for. Alshams.' He held his arms out towards the gate.

'It's down here? But I thought it was the sun's city? There's. . . No sun down here. Is there?'

'Well spotted,' said Hamad sarcastically. 'It'll make sense when we get there.'

Farah didn't move. Hamad took a few steps forward. Farah remained rooted to the spot.

'Worse than herding cats,' he muttered.

Farah looked past him to the gate. It was circular, with radiating spikes to resemble the sun.

'So,' Hamad said. 'Can we go now?'

Farah chewed on her lip. 'One more question,' she said, holding a finger up.

Hamad rolled his eyes. 'If it's about the mouse. I told you I –'

'Not about the mouse. How did you know Amira and I were searching for the city?'

Hamad seemed to consider his next words carefully.

'I saw you,' he said at last.

'How?'

Hamad looked confused. 'Through Manayer,' he said, as if this were obvious. The *jinni* ruffled her feathers in response to her name. He stroked her gently, kissing the back of her feathered head. 'Whenever I'm asleep, I see the world through her eyes.'

'When you're asleep?' said Farah slowly, as one piece of the puzzle began to click into place in her mind. She hadn't been sleeping much recently, but when she had, she'd had the same dream over and over, of being buried in sand . . .

Realization prickled at Farah like an electric current. She wasn't being buried. She was seeing Layla crawl through the sand, diving in and out to hunt. She had the same power as Hamad. And it was getting stronger.

'Does that mean you fly everywhere?' she asked. Hamad opened his mouth to answer her question, but she quickly followed with another, and another. 'What's it like? Does it scare you?'

Hamad laughed. 'Which question should I answer first?'

'All of them!'

'I do fly,' Hamad explained. 'It doesn't scare me. Maybe

it did at first, but I'm used to it now. It feels like being weightless, like I'm just floating through the world. It's . . . magic.'

Farah's own experience had been quite different. But maybe now she understood what her dreams were, it would be more fun.

'I only see a few minutes from my *jinni*'s perspective when I'm asleep,' she said. 'How do you see yours for longer?'

'We train our legs to walk, and then run, don't we?'

'I know *that*,' said Farah.

'Magic is the same.'

'Magic is like a muscle?'

'Exactly. Nurture it, and you'll be able to push its limits. It's why I have these goggles.'

Hamad pulled them down, so they covered his eyes. Now all Farah could see reflected back at her was her own face, shimmering in brass.

'What do they do?' Farah asked.

Hamad pulled the goggles off and handed them to her. They had an adjustable brown leather strap that looked a bit like a belt.

'If I clear my mind, and use the goggles, I don't even need to be asleep,' Hamad explained. 'I see everything Manayer sees instead.'

Farah snorted. 'I don't think I've ever had a clear mind. Too many curiosities to figure out. And anyway, when my mind *is* clear, Layla turns invisible.'

Hamad grinned. 'That's funny. Mine is the opposite. Manayer comes to me when I feel calm.' He held the goggles out for Farah to try them on.

She put them over her eyes, and concentrated on being calm. She took a deep breath and released it slowly, letting her thoughts fly out of her body. But immediately she thought of Amira up in the desert, and Namur, and her sister. And instead of seeing through Layla's eyes, all Farah could see through the goggles was a haze of darkness.

'It doesn't work for me,' she said sulkily, handing Hamad the goggles back. 'Anyway, it still doesn't explain how you knew Amira and I were searching for the city.'

'Nothing gets past you, does it?' remarked Hamad. 'Well, as soon Manayer and I found one another, for the first time I felt a pull to the world above. It was unfamiliar to me, not anything I had ever desired before.'

Farah nodded along. She had felt a pull to the desert her entire life. At first she'd thought it was because she sought adventure. But she understood, now, it was the *jinn* seeking one another out. How else did she happen to cross Amira and Leo's paths in all of Sahar? And how else had they found one another? Farah could say it was fate, or a joint desire to save the world, but it was deeper than that. A feeling that couldn't be ignored. And now she had found Hamad too.

'Have you been able to feel other people's emotions?' Farah asked. Amira's powers hadn't strengthened in the same way as Farah's, but maybe Hamad's had.

Hamad frowned. 'I . . . No. I can't do any of that,' he said. But he was looking at Farah a little differently now.

'What?' Farah said, feeling a little alarmed.

Hamad laughed. 'Sorry. I've just never met someone else with a *jinni* before,' he said.

'You mean Moonchild?' said Farah. 'That's what we call ourselves.'

'I like that. It sounds important. Well, Moonchild, shall we go to the city?'

Farah turned back again, as if expecting Amira to

appear behind her.

'You can't go back until sunrise,' Hamad reminded her.

Farah sighed. She could either stand here for the entirety of the long night, or go into the city Teta had told her about, and figure out a way to bring the sun back for good. 'Fine,' she said at last. Layla nuzzled into her hair, comforting her.

It was tough losing Amira on top of everything else. But Farah had to put that out of her mind for now. So she buried it, along with her other worries. She was so full of them now that she felt as if she might explode.

As they approached the gates, the spikes representing the sun's rays slid back, one by one, until all that faced them was a circle of gold. And, of its own accord, the gate swung open, splitting the circle in two.

Chapter 16

The tunnel that had led to the gate was unassuming, carved from sand and rock. But here, it was different. The floor was made of marble that looked like white clouds against a pink sky; the walls were dotted with gold that shimmered in the darkness like twinkling stars.

Ahead, Farah could see tall spires, and hear rippling water far below. She walked to the very edge of a golden balcony, her eyes widening as she gazed out at the city of Alshams.

This was the place Teta Nourah had told her about. It had been real, all along. Something inside Farah stirred, like waking up after a long sleep. How had Teta known about this place? And had she told Farah about it for a reason? Was it like Alhitan, or different?

A spacious cavern ten times the size of Farah's village at home lay before her. A river surrounded the city below.

Carved into the walls at the end nearest to them were neat, square houses, each one the same. They bundled together like a family of mice, hiding from the winter.

'This is amazing!' said Farah. 'I've never seen a city like it.'

Below, people darted around like ants. Farah could smell their emotions from way up here, and had to work hard not to let them overpower her. Layers of fruit, cream, burning, cooking, oil and fire, spices and herbs mingled into one, giving her a headache.

The place where the sky should have been was coated in darkness, like a starless, moonless night. Hamad explained that the cavern went all the way up until it reached the desert. But how far, then, had Farah fallen?

The city didn't need the sun or moon for light; it was almost as if it *was* the sun. The buildings glowed golden, shining a yellow haze of warmth on everything. That same warmth seemed to soak into Farah's bones, but then she realized she was absorbing Hamad's calmness.

Farah spent some moments staring into the distance . . . before the ground below her rumbled and quaked.

'It's not happening again is it?' Farah asked, thinking

back to the house in the desert. She wasn't sure she could handle more structures crumbling from under her. Particularly as they were standing way up high.

Hamad laughed. 'It's a moving platform.'

Farah realized their balcony was slowly moving downwards. She leaned over the balustrade as the city grew closer, feeling for a moment as if she was flying.

'Amazing!' she exclaimed.

'If you think *this* is amazing,' said Hamad, 'wait until we get inside the Sundial.'

He pointed straight ahead to a grand building that stood at the very centre of the city, and appeared to be its source of light. It resembled the rising sun, like the gate but on a larger scale. Spires like sun rays shot up into the darkness. Like earth with the sun, everything in the city faced the Sundial: the houses standing across the river, adjacent to the balcony they were on, and the city buildings behind. At its heart was a burning ball of fire that flickered red, orange and yellow.

'The Sundial,' Hamad told Farah, 'stores all of our magic, drawing light from the sun. It's the heart of Alshams. Our lifeblood.'

Chapter 17

As they crossed a bridge into the city towards the Sundial, Farah peered into the river, entranced.

'What are they?' she asked. 'They're . . . glowing.'

'Jellyfish,' Hamad explained.

Farah could see jellyfish swimming over one another, darting around other neon-coloured fish. The water seemed impossibly deep, just as the ceiling seemed impossibly high. For a world buried beneath the sands, Alshams felt boundless, like the sea.

'They look like stars, but in the water, not the sky,' Farah mused. She could have stayed there all day, watching the jellyfish ebb and flow, but they had more important matters to settle.

People bustled around, the doors of their homes wide open, moving furniture and goods outside.

'Where are they all going?' asked Farah.

Hamad pursed his lips, as if he didn't want to answer.

'Nowhere. Not yet, anyway.'

'You're going to have to explain more than that,' Farah said. She folded her arms. 'Or I won't follow you inside.'

Hamad sighed. 'They're packing to leave,' he said. 'As you know, the only way in and out of the city is through the tunnel we just came through. Once the sun disappears for good, we're stuck here. So we're all getting ready to move into the desert, just in case.'

'Will that really happen?' asked Farah. She knew the days were growing shorter, but she hadn't expected they would extinguish altogether, like a dying fire. Her eyes scanned dozens, perhaps hundreds of people, including children.

'It won't happen,' Hamad answered with certainty. 'Because we have a plan.'

They were standing outside the Sundial now. Hamad placed his hands on the gilded double doors. 'Now, do you want to find out how to restore the sun, or not?'

Farah could sense his impatience, taking over the calm. Mingled with her own curiosity, it was electrifying. 'Of course,' she said, and she followed him through the doors and into a bustling foyer.

Dozens of people darted around like bees in a hive. A few nodded at Hamad. All of them wearing a variation of his clothing. The walls were covered in intricately painted blue tiles, and the ceiling was bowl-shaped, decorated with a mural of the sun.

Layla darted down Farah's arm, wrapping her tail around her wrist, as Hamad led Farah through a pair of wooden doors beside a set of sweeping stairs, and into a room the size of Amira's dhow.

Low sofas lined the walls, covered in red and brown

patterns. Behind the sofas hung golden curtains draped to a marbled floor that matched the path to the city. At the centre of it all was an enormous rug in the same pattern as the sofas, housing a long gold table that stood with a pot of tea and clear glass teacups waiting to be poured.

Seated, at the far corner, was a woman with brown skin and white hair. As they approached, she smiled at Hamad, before her eyes rested on Farah.

'Nourah?' said the woman, placing a hand to her mouth. 'Is it really you?'

Hamad seemed confused. Manayer flew from his arm and landed on a perch nearby.

'N-no,' said Farah, her gut wrenching at the name. A strange sensation coursed through her veins as her world cracked open like an egg. 'I'm not Nourah. That was . . . my teta. I'm Farah.' Trying to keep her voice and nerves steady, she turned to Hamad, silently asking him for the woman's name.

But the woman answered first. 'I'm Shurooq,' she said with a smile. 'I am sorry to surprise you like that. It's just . . . I heard of her passing, and for a moment, I thought

I was looking at a ghost.'

'You knew her?' asked Farah, though that much was already clear.

'Please, take a seat,' Shurooq said. She poured three cups of saffron-scented tea. 'Hamad, will you find something for Farah's hand?'

Hamad disappeared off into a side room and returned with gauze and some ointment. Farah tried to ignore the pain as he cleaned the wound and then applied the medicine. She felt the weight of Layla shift in her hair, comforting her.

'Your teta lived here for some years when she was younger,' Shurooq explained. 'Before she had her son. We worked together. She was my closest friend for a time.'

Farah couldn't believe it. Teta hadn't just *heard* about the city – she had been a part of it. There was so much more to the woman she had only known as her grandmother.

'Was she born here?' she asked.

'No,' said Shurooq, taking a quick sip of tea, steam billowing from her cup. 'I travelled a bit in my youth and we met by chance. And, well . . . that was that. She became one of us.'

Being around Shurooq was like being swept into a cloud. Where Hamad made Farah feel warm, Shurooq sent an exciting chill through her – like stepping outside on a fresh morning, the day full of possibilities. Is that why Teta had become friends with her? Farah knew she could trust anyone her grandmother had cared about.

'Are you . . . the queen?' Farah asked, suddenly aware of the grandeur of her surroundings.

Shurooq cackled. The sound was croaky; full of joy. 'Oh my, how grand that sounds. No. We don't believe in blood rulers here. We vote.'

'Vote?' Farah echoed.

Hamad nodded. 'We choose our rulers.'

'In the same way,' Shurooq added, 'anyone can perform sun magic, not just the chosen few.'

Farah thought this over. She'd found herself thrust into a life of magic, sometimes unwillingly, and she had felt, many times, unprepared. There was something about being able to *learn* magic, practise it the way Hamad had described, that seemed exciting.

'So, tell me,' said Shurooq, watching Farah closely. 'What did your teta teach you about sun magic?'

Farah told the story she had shared with Amira, about the moon and the sun and the cities they had ruled. 'Even though I'd been to Alhitan, I wasn't sure it was real until . . . well, now,' she admitted.

Hamad finished wrapping up Farah's wound. Though it stung, Farah felt a little better. The tea had helped too. The throbbing in her shoulder was beginning to fade, and she could move it without much trouble.

'I don't understand why the city is down here,' said Farah, her curiosity making her braver. 'In Teta's story, she said the sun didn't like to hide. Why, then, is Alshams hidden like Alhitan?'

'Clever girl,' Shurooq said, sounding impressed. 'Well, there's a little more to the story, you see.'

She patted the seat next to her; Farah slid closer, ready to drink in her words.

'Long ago,' began Shurooq, 'the Sun and the Moon were angry.'

The Legend of the City of Alshams

The Sun and the Moon were angry at the selfishness of their people, which had grown and spread like a disease. And so, to show them the path to kindness, they set a series of trials.

Three, to be exact.

These were no ordinary tasks. Each was designed to address a different trait: ignorance, apathy and greed. The people of the Moon passed their tasks, and so they returned to their lives. But the people of the Sun struggled a little more.

The first task was straightforward enough. Every person – young and old – was given a seed to nuture. What the people did not know was that these were no ordinary seeds. For every day the plants were ignored, their roots grew deeper and firmer.

Only half of the Sun's people passed the first task.

For the rest, soon the roots of their plants spread, cracking the pots they were in, growing from the floor to the ceiling. Eventually they even outgrew their houses, their stems crushing buildings like they were nothing but chicken eggs.

Those who had forgotten to nurture their plants – those who showed ignorance – were forced to watch their houses crumble, before fleeing to seek shelter. Those remaining – those who had diligently looked after their plants so they grew normally – were afraid.

They ignored the knocks of those who had lost their homes, and told them to seek shelter elsewhere. They remained selfish, too busy trying to look after their own needs, too busy trying to pass the tasks set by the Sun and Moon, to help their friends.

The Sun was disappointed. The first task had not gone to plan.

As time passed, the fear and selfishness of the Sun's people bred apathy. They no longer thought about their friends or cared what happened to them.

What they did not realize was the second task was already under way. And it was a trick. To pass the second task, you had to open your home to a friend in need, not turn your back. And so those who had looked after their own plants, but ignored those who cried for help, had failed this task too.

Only one of the contestants made it through to the final task. A fisherman with a young family, who had opened his home to a different neighbour on every night of the week. He fed them, clothed them, and offered them shelter.

The final task was trickiest of all, though it offered a reward: a coin the size of your palm, which shone golden like the sun on one side and silver like the moon on the other. It would grant a wish to any who came across it, and was given by the Sun and the Moon themselves.

But the coin was locked in a chest filled with sand, buried at the bottom of a deep, pearlescent lake. When the fisherman heard of the final task, he was pleased. He thought it would be easy. After all, it was his job to row out into the lake from morning until night to gather fish to sell to his village. He knew it as well as he knew his family.

But the fisherman hadn't anticipated the challenges that lay ahead.

The lake, which had previously contained only fish, was now home to monsters. Serpents that swam beneath the boat, their bodies slick and cold, threatening to capsize it; hands that seemed to belong to decaying bodies reaching out of the water, begging to be let aboard. And strange whispers pierced the silence, warning the fisherman to turn back.

But he didn't listen. He was determined to get his wish.

After twelve days and twelve nights the fisherman finally managed to pull the chest from the lake. He took it back to his wife and son, and they opened it together.

Inside the chest was a village made of sand, an exact replica of their own. The fisherman could even see his family through the tiny window of his home, and the people from his village walking around, chatting together.

But in order to reach the coin, the Sun and the Moon explained, the fisherman had to crush the village and all who lived there. And whatever he did inside the chest would happen in real life.

In order to wish on the coin, the fisherman would have to flip it and pick a side. If it landed and he guessed correctly, his wish would be granted. If he guessed incorrectly, he would have to sacrifice something greater in return.

'Don't fear,' said the fisherman to his wife. 'I can wish for the village to be rebuilt. We can then sell the coin and live the rest of our lives like royalty.'

'But what if it doesn't work?' asked the wife.

'Then you take the next wish,' said the fisherman. 'The coin grants a wish to any who comes across it. We have one each.'

The wife spent a day and a night trying to persuade her husband not to go through with it. But she failed. The very next day the family took the chest out into the lake in the fisherman's boat, and the fisherman reached his hand inside the chest for the coin.

The family watched from the boat as their village crumbled, the villagers screaming and running for their lives. Some made it into the lake, where they were consumed by the serpents and the strange, skeletal monsters. Others were buried alive in the sand.

With the chaos raging around him, the fisherman flipped the coin and called confidently for the Sun. But when it landed in his outstretched hand, he saw, shining back at him, the Moon.

He turned in his boat to face his family, to ask his wife to make the next wish.

But they too were gone.

In his search for riches, he had forgotten the most important thing: the sacrifice that he would have to make.

'Where are they?' the fisherman asked the Sun and the Moon. 'Where have they gone?'

But he had lost the gamble.

Every day for the rest of his life, the fisherman rowed out to the place where he had last seen his wife and son. Sometimes he thought he heard his wife and son call for him. On rare occasions, he saw skeletal hands reach for him – and he could swear they belonged to his family. He tried to pull them on to the boat, but they disappeared.

Years later, when the fisherman was old and tired of searching, he threw the coin into the lake, hoping no one would find it and curse themselves as he had. He rowed back to land, and did not turn to see the lake sink into the depths of the desert to join the village that had crumbled around it. Then he walked towards the horizon, leaving nothing behind but bad decisions and long-lost memories.

Or so he thought.

Chapter 18

As Shurooq told her story, Farah understood, now, why Teta had mentioned a city that 'appeared' where the sun shone hottest . . . Because it wasn't always there. She also understood why no one in the world above spoke of it . . . They didn't know it existed. But she still didn't understand what they needed to do to restore the sun as the long nights continued to lengthen. She couldn't let the people of Alshams lose their homes; couldn't let the world above die because she and her friends had released Moon magic into the world.

'Now,' Shurooq said, finishing her tea, 'it's your turn.'

'What do you mean?' asked Farah, shifting uncomfortably.

'We were very surprised when Manayer flew into our lives some months ago, as you can imagine,' said Shurooq. 'And even more surprised when we heard reports of the sun disappearing. I'm assuming you and your friends had something to do with this?'

Farah nodded, feeling ashamed. She told Shurooq and Hamad about Alhitan, and how she, Amira and Leo had released all of the *jinn*. 'I'm sorry,' she finally said. 'We didn't mean to make everything worse. We were trying to save Alhitan, and stop the world from being destroyed by the stormbird . . .'

But when Farah glanced up at Shurooq, she wasn't met by the resentment she was expecting.

'What are you sorry for?' asked Shurooq kindly.

'For cursing you!' exclaimed Farah. 'And ruining the world!'

Shurooq and Hamad glanced at one another, and laughed.

Farah was confused by their reaction. 'I . . . Why is this funny?'

'Oh, habibti,' said Shurooq, clasping Farah's hands in hers. Farah breathed in her sweet scent. 'It's quite the opposite.'

Farah was even more confused now. 'I don't understand. If the sun is disappearing and the moon is taking over, isn't that going to destroy the world? I don't see how that's the opposite of ruining everything.'

Shurooq raised her eyebrows at Hamad. 'I see you explained nothing to the poor child before you brought her here,' she scolded.

'It was hard to know where to start,' said a flustered Hamad. 'And she had that bite. I was more concerned about it getting infected. If the ro—'

'We'll move on to that in a moment,' said Shurooq, waving Hamad away. 'My goodness, you do like to jump ahead.'

Hamad scowled. 'This is why I thought *you* should tell her.'

'And so I will,' teased Shurooq, 'if you'll be quiet for a moment. In fact, why don't you go and prepare us some food? Make yourself useful.'

Their bickering reminded Farah of her relationship with Amira, and she felt a pang, realizing now that it was sometimes a sign of love. It meant that you were close enough to someone to tell them all of your thoughts.

'Now,' said Shurooq, turning her attention to Farah again as Hamad left the room. 'Let me give you a tour while I share my next story.'

She glided out of the room like a bird in flight. Farah could smell her determination; see it seeping out of her like light. And she followed, like a moth to a flame.

'I'm afraid we're going to have to be quick,' explained Shurooq, leading the way up the sweeping staircase Farah had seen earlier. The foyer was now empty, like being at school after the last bell had rung. Eerie, ghostly. 'The magic is running out and we have a lot to do in a short space of time.'

A balcony at the top of the stairs overlooked the foyer. Lining the walls were objects encased in glass.

'This allows you to see into the past,' explained Shurooq, opening one of the glass doors with a pair of keys around her neck. She took out an object which resembled a mirror, but instead of her own reflection, Farah could see the room beyond.

'How?' asked Farah leaning in for a closer look.

'The world leaves a record of everything left behind. Memories which, if properly stored, can be replayed.'

'But how was it made?'

'Through years of record-keeping, preserving moments, and practice, to make the glass reflect just right. It would be a shame to lose it, along with one thousand years of research . . .'

Shurooq suddenly smelled like rotting fruit, sickly sweet on Farah's tongue. It reminded Farah of Teta before she had passed.

'Why can't you take it with you?' Farah asked.

'Because this is the home of the sun,' said Shurooq. 'To abandon it would be to abandon the magic she gifted us. Just as the *jinn* were born in Alhitan, so too was our magic born here.'

Farah nodded, trying to understand. 'Can I try? Have a look through the mirror?'

'Of course.' Shurooq adjusted a set of dials on the side of the mirror. 'I often go back to this one,' she said, her voice soft.

Through the mirror, Farah saw groups of people chatting to one another. It was morning, and things were busy in the Sundial.

A young woman rushed inside, her hair tied up into a nest, strands falling at her face. She looked up at the balcony and waved with a smile. Teta. Down the stairs towards her ran a young Shurooq. As they met and whispered together, Shurooq clasped Teta's hand in hers and they hurried to another room. Silent tears slid down Farah's face as she watched them, so full of excitement and hope. Seeing Teta now, Farah knew she couldn't let her down. Layla stretched her claws, reminding Farah she was there with her.

Roughly wiping her tears away, Farah turned back to Shurooq and focused on the task at hand. 'This is like my friend's map box,' she said. 'When we were searching for Alshams we knew we needed the hottest point in the desert, and so Amira turned back time to see where the sun fell in the middle of the day. She's done it before, with the moon . . .'

Shurooq was impressed by their methods, but unsurprised by their contraption. 'Our magic, based on logic, makes it out into the world. It's partly what keeps us going. That's one example of how sun magic is open to anyone who wants to practise it.'

'Can you do the same with moon magic?' asked Farah. 'Put it inside something so anyone can use it?'

'Yes,' said Shurooq. 'If you have moondust at your disposal. Though I'm afraid that's much harder to find than our source of magic. It comes only from the *jinn* realm.'

Shurooq led them down the long hall and towards an opening right at the centre of the Sundial. 'Here we are,' she said, holding out her arms. 'The source of our magic. Sun rays.'

Inside the room was the great fireball Farah had seen when she had first entered Alshams. Up close, she could see it was encased in glass. Farah was unable to look directly at the fireball without it hurting her eyes.

Beyond the fireball was a window that spanned several floors. From here, Farah could see the houses beyond the river.

'In the story, there was a lake. It's just a river now,' Farah observed.

Shurooq nodded. 'The houses you see were what existed before. We didn't need this,' she said, glancing at the ball of fire, 'because we had access to the sun. Over the years, we learned to be clever with our magic, and built on top of the lake.'

Every person in Alshams faced the Sundial. They could all see their magic, and watch as it slowly faded with the sun. The very base of the glass encasing the fireball was coated with a thick layer of brass. Farah was reminded of Hamad's goggles.

'We preserve the sun's magic with brass,' explained Shurooq. 'Too much, and it stops it. Just enough, and you can control its direction. Moon magic uses brass too. It's why *jinn* bottles are made of brass.'

'How do you collect the rays?'

'Sunseekers travel on rotation to gather energy from the sun,' said Shurooq. 'As they do, they trade goods, and keep the magic of our world ticking over.'

Farah thought about Amira's map box. It was clear, now, how the sun magic had landed in her mothers' hands.

'But with the sun sparse, the Sunseekers are beginning to return without much to pass along,' Shurooq continued. 'And this, unfortunately, is all we have left after the long nights.'

Farah fell silent. She had hoped to be inspired by Shurooq's tour, but instead she felt deflated. 'So this *is* our fault,' she said at last. 'We cursed your world, and the one above!'

'That is a little dramatic,' said Shurooq calmly. 'Now that you understand how our magic works, let me tell you about the Moon and the Sun's very first mistake. It happened long before they set the three challenges . . .

The Moon and the Sun's First Mistake

The Moon and the Sun had enjoyed many years together, their love for one another creating a balance and harmony in the world. And perhaps, a little naively, they had assumed that harmony would remain.

Every day the Sun woke and set to work. She would light up the earth, warm it, and help all that lived on the planet thrive and grow. The earth orbited the Sun, fawning over her power, and in truth, made the Moon a little jealous. So, every once in a while, the Moon would remind the earth of her role. She alone had the power to separate the earth from the Sun with a solar eclipse, and she made her strengths known, so the earth would fear her.

But the Sun loved the Moon for her strengths and her versatility. For without her, the earth would slow, the tides would change, and the seasons, as we know them, would shift.

Just as their lives intertwined, as did their magic.

And so, with sun magic removed from the Sahar Peninsula at the hands of a greedy fisherman who had wished on a coin, the Moon offered the Sun a solution. The Moon's children would gather their *jinn* and go on a journey to unlock the magic from the Sun's city, cursed to live beneath the sands.

But the Moon and the Sun had underestimated the fear that lies within people, and the lengths they will go to in order to keep control. The Moon and the Sun did not intend for moon magic to be cursed; they did not expect Alhitan to be encased in brass to stop the magic flowing. But it happened all the same. And so the Moon and the Sun watched, helpless, as Alhitan was attacked, with catapults of molten brass; they watched as the city was coated, its magic trapped; and they watched as it sank into the depths of the ocean, its people frozen in time for a thousand years.

Until two sea witches had released three *jinn* into the world: a cat, a lizard and a fish.

Chapter 19

'I believe you know the rest of the story,' said Shurooq. 'You lived it, after all.'

She led Farah back down the stairs and into the empty foyer. Farah followed silently, soaking in Shurooq's words. She had thought they – the Moonchildren – had ruined the balance of the world by freeing the *jinni*. She had been carrying the guilt around, like rocks in her stomach. But now she finally understood.

'So,' began Farah. 'We *needed* to release moon magic into the world?'

'That's right.'

'And all of this wasn't our fault? There's just . . . a second part to our mission?'

'Exactly.'

Relief flooded through Farah like butterflies in spring. The guilt she had been carrying around fluttered away.

Upon entering the main room where Hamad and

Manayer were waiting for them, Farah recognized the smell instantly.

'Majboos!' she said in delight.

On the table was a platter, with raisins shining like jewels amidst the saffron-soaked rice and glistening chicken. Hamad served them each a plate, and they took a break from their discussion to enjoy their food.

The first bite was the best. Farah had eaten dates for so long that she'd almost forgotten what a full meal tasted like. The flavours exploded in her mouth, and she sat for a moment, intent on filling her belly. She couldn't help thinking how much Namur would have enjoyed the chicken, and Amira the rice. And even though she knew she couldn't reach them yet, she put a portion aside, just in case.

Settling down to another cup of steaming tea, Shurooq turned to Farah. 'Your friend Amira,' she began. 'Where is she now?'

'Still in the desert,' Farah explained, pushing down the worries that her friend was alone. 'We were separated when I entered the building.'

Shurooq's face turned serious, and she nodded along

as Farah described the mouse, and how her curiosity had taken over.

'That brings us to my next question,' Shurooq said. 'Apart from the mouse, have any other creatures followed you in the desert?'

Farah frowned. 'Well . . . yes. A snake. But we got rid of it.'

Shurooq shook her head. 'Trust me, you didn't. And you don't want to either.'

Farah waited for Shurooq to continue.

'The creature that bit you, and the other that chased you through the desert – those are rogue *jinn*.'

Farah remembered how the snake glowed in the moonlight. She hadn't thought of it then because *jinn* are meant to be invisible without a human. 'A snake and a mouse . . . Those were two *jinn* released from the bottles!'

Shurooq nodded. 'When you released them all, they, like Manayer, went in search of a human. But the long nights have confused them.'

'Why?' asked Farah.

'Think about your connection to the *jinn* realm. Has it become stronger?'

Farah nodded, and glanced at Hamad. 'Yes. I've started to see things through Layla's eyes. That never happened before. And I can feel everyone's emotions, not just smell or see them.' Being around Hamad made her feel calm, just as being around Amira made her passionate. Her moods were shifting into theirs, as if she carried their joys and burdens.

'Feel them, you say?' said Shurooq, raising her eyebrows at Hamad.

'Yes,' said Farah. 'Why?'

Shurooq shook her head, as if freeing herself from a daze. And then she continued to explain. 'The *jinn* realm is tearing open, like a loose seam. And the rogue *jinn* can't see through the fog to find their humans.'

Farah frowned. 'But I thought the whole *point* was to release emotions, to make sure the stormbird didn't return?'

'You need balance,' explained Shurooq. 'Emotions are powerful, essential to our world. But without logic, without a way to steer them they –'

'Get out of control,' Farah finished.

Everyone fell silent for a moment. Layla scuttled over

the table and drank a few drops of tea that had dripped into the saucer.

'So the *jinn* are running rogue, and we need to stop them, like we did the stormbird?' said Farah at last.

'Not quite,' said Shurooq, while Hamad fiddled with the flute at his belt.

'But the mouse tried to take Layla,' Farah insisted. 'Why would it hurt one of its own? We *have* to stop them.'

Shurooq sighed. 'Rogue *jinn* are different. Without a human, they follow their emotions freely. Think of Layla, who only appears when you're curious. If she were rogue, she would scuttle around everywhere, her curiosity getting her in trouble. And she would be stronger for it too, her powers concentrated.'

Farah frowned. 'But I thought *jinn* were good,' she said.

'It's not that straightforward,' explained Shurooq patiently. 'All of us have good *and* bad inside us. We have to work hard to remain good.'

'So what do we need to do?' asked Farah, beginning to feel helpless. If she and her friends were responsible for the rogue *jinn*, she needed to do something about them!

Shurooq looked at Farah. 'What do you think you

need to do?' she asked.

Farah thought of Layla, and Namur, and Semek and Manayer, and how precious they all were. She thought of the bond they shared with their Moonchildren, and how it was unlike any other. And she thought of balance, harmony, everything Hamad and Shurooq had been saying. And suddenly it hit her like a gust of wind, making her stand up abruptly, her plate clattering to the ground.

'We need to guide them,' she said. 'To find their people.'

Shurooq grinned widely. 'There is a way to do this. Hamad will show you tomorrow. But in order to release sun magic into the world, we need *all* of the *jinn*. We need them to enter Alshams, like you and Layla did.'

Farah sat back down. She tried to remember all of the *jinn* they had released from the bottles. There was the snake, the mouse, and Manayer. With Namur and Layla that made five. What about the other two? And Semek? He had disappeared after Leo went missing. 'Could some of the others have found a human?' she asked.

'It would be unlikely, with emotions running wild the way they are.' Shurooq exchanged another glance with

Hamad. 'So we must tread carefully. The more of you that are down here, the more the rogue *jinn* will be drawn to this place. You are all connected to one another, like opposite sides of a magnet.'

Farah thought back to the snake. She tried to work out what emotion it was feeling out there in the desert. It seemed monstrous, evil. But, as Amira said, even villains have their own story to tell. What was the snake's story?

'How will they come down here?' Farah asked. 'The building only appears during the day, and the *jinn* disappear at the end of every night.'

'There is a moment, a small window, where the sun and moon share space in the sky. That's when they will take their chance.'

Farah's mind was whirring as she tried to piece together what they had to do: attract a group of rogue *jinn* and save the city of Alshams from crumbling. It seemed impossible. What about Leo's missing *jinni*, Semek? What about the other *jinn* they hadn't even seen? And how in Sahar were they to stop the rogue *jinni* from attacking them?

Farah had one final question. 'What happens if we fail?'

Farah could smell Shurooq's sweetness turn sour before the woman spoke her next words.

'The days will continue to grow shorter until the sun stops appearing at all. When that happens, we'll be here permanently. And when our store of sun magic runs out, the city will crumble like a sandcastle.'

Chapter 20

Shurooq showed Farah to her room. Hamad had already left, having agreed to meet Farah in the morning to discuss the rogue *jinn*.

'These apartments belong to the leader of Alshams. Hundreds lived here before me, each one leaving something behind,' she explained. 'There are two rooms – one for guests – and a bathroom between them. Over there is the kitchen. Take what you need.'

'Thank you,' said Farah, drinking in Shurooq's kindness. 'Where does Hamad stay?'

'At home,' explained Shurooq, stifling a yawn. 'I'm sorry, but I'm quite tired. I've been monitoring the town over the last few days, making sure everyone is packed and ready to go. Your arrival changes things for the better, of course, but we still need to be careful.'

Farah thought back to all the people she had seen, packing up their worldly possessions. She knew well what it was like to leave home in a hurry. She didn't quite understand how her being here could change things so much, but she supposed she would find out tomorrow. She had asked enough questions for one day.

As she crawled into the cool sheets, Farah could feel Amira's absence beside her. They had slept tucked up together in Amira's tiny cabin for months, and then in the sprawling desert. It was odd to be alone with Layla.

Eventually, though she couldn't pinpoint exactly when, Farah fell into a deep sleep.

Later, during the long night, Farah dreamed of gold and luminescent fish, as Layla took her on an adventure unlike any they had experienced before. Now she knew she was seeing the world from Layla's perspective, Farah found it exciting. She could see clearer in the shadows, everything just a little bit brighter.

The *jinni* scuttled down the side of the Sundial and out on to the cold ground. Everyone else was asleep. It was so quiet you could hear the gentle ripple of water from the river.

Layla peered into the water, where the jellyfish swam

together, dipping her nose in to test it before leaping in. Farah could feel her lizard's arms work as she glided through the river like a bird in flight. It was like swimming through the stars, darkness and light blending into one. Layla's feet propelled her through the water as she dived between rocks, to find shining pearls in the deep, resurfacing for moments to catch her breath before diving in once more.

After that, they wandered the city, passing empty spires that glistened in the dark like gems. They stood behind the Sundial, as if following it into battle. The battle they had planned wasn't like the ones you hear about in stories. It wasn't about good and evil, but about restoring balance. Somehow, that made it all the more difficult.

Later, Layla returned to nuzzle Farah's hair, and Farah's dreams turned to shadows, wrapping themselves around her like a warm blanket on a cold night.

When Farah entered the kitchen the next day she found Hamad there, on his own, his back to her. She seated herself at a chair, a spread of bread and cheese on the table.

'Morning,' she said, smiling a little when Hamad jumped.

He glared at her. 'You scuttle around like your lizard. How are you so good at moving unseen?'

'Magic,' joked Farah, but the truth was she had lots of practice. Sneaking out at night so your parents couldn't hear required a soft tread, and she was used to shrinking herself into small spaces, so as not to be a nuisance.

'Did you sleep well?' asked Hamad.

Farah smiled. 'Layla took me on an adventure.' And she told him about their trip around the city, and how peaceful everything was at night.

Hamad took the flute from his belt and placed it on the table. Farah could feel it hum, the vibrations making the cups and plates wobble.

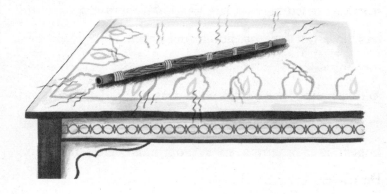

'When this is all over, I'll give you a proper tour,' Hamad said, taking a bite of bread.

'How can you be sure there will be anything left?' asked Farah. She found his optimism a little annoying.

'Because I believe in you,' Hamad said casually.

His words burrowed deep. Farah pulled a face. 'What does that mean?'

Hamad pushed the flute towards Farah. She stared at it, confused.

'What is this for?' she said.

'Pick it up,' said Hamad, pushing it a little further.

Farah rolled her eyes. Hamad never gave straight answers. For a curious mind, this was infuriating. She reached for the flute, allowing the hum to work its way up her arm and into her bones. It reminded her of the stormbird's energy, of Amira's bakhoor pot. The flute had holes all the way along one side, and a shiny brass mouthpiece. Farah thought back to what Shurooq had told her about brass trapping magic.

'You're supposed to cover the holes with the top three fingers of each hand, and breathe into the mouthpiece,' Hamad explained.

Farah did as instructed, but nothing happened. All she could hear was her own breath moving through the instrument like she was letting out a long sigh.

'Am I doing it wrong?' Farah asked.

'Yes and no,' Hamad said.

Farah paused. 'Is this supposed to be a riddle?'

Hamad laughed. 'For now, all you need to know is that the instrument holds both sun and moon magic inside. It –'

'How does it hold both kinds of magic?' interrupted Farah.

Hamad smiled again in a way that annoyed Farah, and she let herself drink some of his calmness for a moment. 'It's all in the making of the instrument, which I'll tell you about in a moment. But what I need to tell you *first* is that it's your job to learn to play this flute.'

Farah paused. 'My job is to play a musical instrument while moon magic slowly kills the earth?'

Hamad shrugged. 'When you put it that way, yes. This isn't just a normal instrument, as you've gathered. If you learn to play it, you can bind the rogue *jinn* to you, and eventually steer them.'

Farah thought about this; about everything Shurooq had explained last night. They had to enlist the rogue *jinn*'s help to return sun magic to the world. But the mouse had snatched Layla, and the snake had attacked her and Amira. Farah wasn't sure she wanted those *jinn* following her around.

'Why would I want to bind violent animals to me?' asked Farah.

'Because once they're paired with you, they'll act differently, like our *jinn*. And, as Shurooq said, we need all of the *jinn* to release moon magic into the world.'

Manayer flapped her wings and cawed. Hamad glanced at her, his brow furrowing, his concern wafting lightly across the room to Farah like the lingering scent of freshly baked goods gone stale.

'What's wrong?' asked Farah.

'She wants to hunt,' explained Hamad. 'But we have to wait until the sun comes up. There's no other way out or in.'

After a bit of fussing, Manayer settled down again, and Hamad brought his attention back to Farah.

'Why do *I* have to play this thing?' Farah asked. She

had wanted to take charge, had wanted to lead like Amira did, but now it seemed like a big weight on her shoulders alone. What if she couldn't do it? 'Why not you, or Shurooq, or someone else?'

'Because it requires someone versed in both sun and moon magic.'

'But *you* are,' countered Farah. 'You grew up here and have your own *jinni*.'

'Unfortunately,' said Hamad, 'I'm not. Not in the way *you* are. I have been raised, all of my life, to believe in emotionless logic. My *jinni* comes to me when I'm feeling calm. *That* I can master. Other emotions . . . the difficult ones, I struggle with. Not like you. You seem to know everyone, *see* everyone for who they truly are, beyond what your *jinni* shows you. That's unique.'

'Is that why you and Shurooq were acting strange when I said I could feel other people's emotions?'

'Yes,' Hamad admitted. 'Your friend Amira, can she do the same?'

Farah shook her head. 'I don't think so. But over the last few days, I seem to be able to let people's emotions in and out too, where before I couldn't control it. Your calmness, Shurooq's kindness. It helps me. But everyone's worries . . . they weigh me down.'

'This is good,' said Hamad. 'You're already training without even realizing it!'

Farah thought about how she could see beyond Amira's anger, and Leo's nerves, and even Hamad's calm exposure. And Hamad was right; it wasn't because Layla showed her. It was something inside herself. Her curious mind meant she saw everyone as a puzzle to solve. Not for the first time, she wondered: if Amira was fire, and Leo was the ocean, what then was she?

'You need to figure that out too,' said Hamad, when Farah explained her concerns. 'You need to understand the *jinn* and how their emotions relate to you. They won't come if they don't feel a connection.'

Fara looked down at the flute, at its potential, and she knew she held the key to saving the Sahar Peninsula in her hands.

'OK,' she said. 'I'll do it.'

Hamad grinned. 'I can teach you the music, the notes to play. That's the logical sun-magic part. The rest, the moon-magic emotions, has to come from you.'

'When?' As scared as she was, Farah knew she had to try.

'Now,' said Hamad. 'The first thing you need to do when you're faced with a rogue *jinn* is to think about what emotion it represents. Layla comes to you when you're feeling curious; Manayer comes to me when I'm feeling calm. Could you sense any emotion from the mouse?'

Farah thought back to the dhow, when the mouse had nibbled on Amira's slippers, and then in the desert, when it had seized Layla. She'd noticed it then, the smell.

'Burnt milk,' said Farah. 'Mischief.'

Hamad nodded, satisfied. 'Now, next time you see it, you have to act quick. Once the flute is in your hands, you have to close your eyes and imagine a moment in your life when you've been mischievous. Try and *feel* those same emotions. When you do, the flute will play music.'

Farah fiddled with the flute now. It felt light in her hands. 'Is that it?' she said. 'That's all I have to do?'

Hamad raised his eyebrows. 'It's not as easy as it looks. Mischief might come to you, but you have to be prepared for other emotions too. The harder ones. What about the snake? What did that represent?'

Farah frowned. 'I never figured that out,' she said.

'That's OK,' said Hamad. He seemed keen not to waste any time. 'Do you remember the remaining two *jinn* released from the bottles? Do you know what animals they were?'

Farah bit her lip and shook her head. 'I'm sorry,' she said, slumping down in frustration. 'Everything happened so fast, I didn't get a chance. I didn't think I'd need to remember . . .'

Layla glided down from Farah's nest of hair and settled on the table across from her. Watching Layla stare at her, glassy eyes focused, she felt a little better.

'How did you come across this flute, anyway?' she asked Hamad.

'I've been waiting for you to ask,' said Hamad, looking pleased. Farah could sense something more to his emotions. Pride. 'I . . . uh, actually made it.'

Hamad sat down across from Farah with Layla perched between them, and launched into an unexpected story.

The Tale of the Magic-maker's Apprentice

Word had reached Alshams that the remaining five *jinn* locked in their bottles for almost one thousand years had been freed by three children – but only two of those children had returned.

Whispers had started at the midnight souk. Following the stormbird's sudden disappearance, it had been rebuilt, though it was only a shadow of its former glory. Those same whispers sailed across the ocean to the port towns surrounding the desert; and eventually, they had reached the sands.

Whispers, as I'm sure you can imagine, travel quicker than children, which is why the news of the Moonchildren's imminent arrival had reached Alshams before they had. And one creature could travel quicker still: a rogue falcon *jinni*.

The falcon flew across the desert, landing just above

the entrance to Alshams. Those whose job it was to guard the entrance during the brief moments of sun, noticed it linger. And the people of Alshams began to speculate.

'It wants one of us!' said a blacksmith.

'But who?' a teacher echoed. They all hoped to be chosen, like characters from a fairy tale introduced to a new and exciting life.

Over one thousand people lived in the city of Alshams and, over ten days, one hundred at a time would march into the desert just before sunset and wait to meet the falcon when it appeared at night. Each one hoped the falcon would choose it – but each time, it did not.

On and on, the groups marched, back and forth, until the final group waited their turn. Amongst this group was a Magic-maker's apprentice, who had hatched his very own plan. He wasn't one for sitting around and waiting for magic to come to him. Which is why, as it happens, he had chosen this particular trade.

Having saved up all his money, he bought the finest wood he could find and whittled a flute. Next, he moulded a mouthpiece of brass, just the right amount to trap a pinch of magic. Then he coated the flute in sun rays from the store that grew Alshams' crops. This wasn't strictly allowed, but he'd seen enough of his friends steal sun rays for much more trivial objects, such as shoes that could make you run faster, and plants that grew sweets instead of fruit.

As night approached, growing longer as it did, the Magic-maker's apprentice had one ingredient left to find: moondust.

Moondust was difficult to come by, and it was rare, which was why moon magic existed primarily through *jinn*. It is also why the sight of a *jinni* was a cause for great excitement. But the Magic-maker's apprentice knew of one object that stored moondust – it was a gift given one thousand years ago by the king of Alhitan to the ruler of Alshams. A ring, made of ruby.

Luckily for the Magic-maker's apprentice, their current leader was his mother's sister, and he found a reason to visit her one afternoon.

Making excuses to leave his workshop, the Magic-maker's apprentice scuttled between the busy lanes of his city, spires looming over him like pieces on a chessboard. The ground was uneven and, in his rush, he almost tripped a few times. He held the flute in his hands, just as the clock struck five. Only an hour until sunset, until he needed to go to the world above for his chance at securing a *jinn*.

You see, the Magic-maker's apprentice was ambitious. He wanted to be a leader someday, like his aunt. But as Alshams is ruled by vote, not blood, he had to make a name for himself. And this, it seemed, was the perfect chance.

'My goodness, nephew. I don't see you here too often,' said his aunt suspiciously as he entered the Sundial.

The Magic-maker's apprentice watched his aunt pour them both a cup of tea, the ruby ring shining on her finger. He wanted to reach for it, pluck it like an apple from a tree, but he had to remain calm. He looked up at his aunt, and he smiled.

'I . . . Well, I've missed you!' he said, not making a good show of his lie.

His aunt narrowed her eyes. The Magic-maker's apprentice cleared his throat. A full minute of silence passed with his aunt studying him closely.

'What is it you *really* want?' she asked at last.

And so, the Magic-maker's apprentice was forced to tell her the truth.

To his surprise, his aunt agreed to give him the moondust from her ring, on one condition. If his flute worked, and he succeeded in binding the rogue falcon *jinni* to him, he must promise to help her find the rest of the *jinn*.

'The nights grow longer,' she said, her usually calm exterior slipping. 'And without these *jinn*, our city, and our world, will crumble.'

What started as an act of self gain had turned into something much greater.

The Magic-maker's apprentice returned to his workshop, and coated his flute in moondust, until it seeped into the wood, leaving a silver sheen. Then he entered the desert, with ninety-nine of his people. All of them were nervous. But the apprentice had a way of remaining calm, even when nerves threatened to take over.

In the desert twilight, the Magic-maker's apprentice played his flute to the rogue *jinni*. Everyone watched, silent, until his song was done. The notes of his flute danced across the desert, and the falcon shot into the air, dancing with it.

As the falcon *jinni* flew closer to him, the apprentice knew at once she was no longer rogue. She flew, landing heavy on his arm, her feathers glowing in the dark.

'Manayer,' he whispered, with a smile.

And, in that moment, he became a Moonchild.

Chapter 21

When Hamad finished his story, Farah stared at him, mouth agape. Even Layla seemed a little surprised.

'You . . .' She paused. 'You bound yourself to Manayer?'

Hamad nodded.

'Why didn't you tell me sooner?'

He sighed. 'I don't know. We've only just met and I thought you might judge me. Like you and your friends would think I wasn't really one of you.'

Farah frowned, feeling bad for him. 'Of course not,' she said. It was so odd to her that Hamad would worry about fitting in as a Moonchild, when she had always been worried about standing out as one.

'Thank you,' said Hamad, though he didn't quite smile. Something about Manayer was still bothering him, Farah could sense it. It surrounded him like a fog. The falcon had just left to scout the city, and Farah could tell Hamad felt her absence even now.

Hamad had made a promise to Shurooq, and so Farah was going to make one to him.

'Teach me the song,' said Farah, standing up suddenly. 'If we're going *jinn* hunting, I want to be ready.'

Farah could see the fog clear around Hamad, just a little. A shadow of a smile returned. 'Maybe avoid calling it *jinn* hunting,' he said. 'I'm not sure Layla likes that idea.'

'Of course you do, Layla,' said Farah, glancing at her *jinni*. 'We want to hunt that horrible mouse, don't we? The one that ran off with you.'

Layla stuck her tongue out in agreement, and Hamad laughed.

'OK,' he began. 'Now, do you know anything about scales?'

'Lizard scales?' joked Farah. 'Layla leaves them *everywhere*.'

Hamad sighed, shaking his head. 'This is going to be much harder than I first imagined.' But Farah could sense his mood had improved with the focus of a task ahead. 'Let's start at the beginning.'

Later that day, Farah retreated for a bath. She took the flute with her, her mind buzzing with the notes Hamad had taught her. They had practised until her fingers were sore, and she found herself absently tapping the notes to the rhythm she had learned in the bubbles. It felt like progress at a time when she couldn't do anything else. But Farah knew as soon as the sun was up, she'd be out there searching for Amira.

As she dunked her hair into the water, washing out days of sand, she thought about her first long night camping in the desert with Amira. It had been when they weren't ravaged by thirst and hunger, and still hopeful for the adventure ahead. And Farah had shown Amira the inside of her hair nest.

'I don't show it to a lot of people,' Farah had said, jokingly. 'So consider yourself special.'

Amira laughed, and it was like hearing bells ring. Then she squealed in horror. 'There are BUGS in your hair. DECAPITATED BUGS.'

Farah simply shrugged. 'Layla likes the heads the most. She saves the bodies for later.'

That had done nothing to soften Amira's expression.

And Farah had laughed, chasing her around, shaking her hair all over her friend.

As Farah dressed again, she opened the pouch on the underside of her top and tucked the flute safely inside. Something cold and hard was already in there. Pulling it out, Farah inspected it. A coin gilded with silver and gold, one side showing the sun and the other the moon.

Farah gasped, feeling the power of it in her hands. 'How?' she asked, turning to Layla, who was waiting patiently on the towel rail. Layla stuck her tongue out and Farah realized she must have retrieved the coin from the bottom of the river when they went swimming together in her dreams. The coin that had cursed the city and sat there for all of this time

Farah tucked it safely back into her pouch. Its magic crackled, tempting her.

Chapter 22

The first sunrise since Farah had arrived at Alshams approached quickly.

Shurooq had shown Layla a clock-like object, another of their creations similar to Amira's map box, that tracked the sun's movements. It predicted that after another long night, spanning close to eighty hours, the sun would rise and set for the final time. After that, no one, including the remaining *jinn*, could enter or leave the city.

The pressure was on for Farah to perfect the flute and bind the rogue *jinn*, and to find Amira and Namur in time to bring them to the city. They all had to be in the city together for the magic to work, *jinn* and Moonchildren, rogue and otherwise.

The sun rays were running out quickly. Once the size of a house, they had shrunk to the size of a horse. Alshams was growing dark, in both mood and light. If the light disappeared for good, then it was no use having eight *jinn* together. They needed sun rays too, to restore Alshams.

Shurooq spent most of her time helping everyone pack. All the while, Hamad and Farah met at her apartments to practise.

Hamad was trying to help her channel mischief, but Farah had never really been a mischievous child. She was quietly curious. Shy.

'Oh, come *on*,' Hamad had said during their first practice. 'Haven't you ever, I don't know . . . tripped someone up as a joke?'

Farah frowned. 'No,' she said. 'Why would I? That's just mean.'

'What about when I stole sun rays? Anything like that?'

Farah sighed. 'I stole a dhow once,' she said. 'To go to the midnight souk.'

Hamad looked surprised. 'Impressive.'

'But it was for the mermaids,' she added. 'They made me do it, so I don't think it counts.'

By their second practice, the city was showing more signs of damage. The Sundial was turning to ruin, and parts of the river were sinking in. Only the houses furthest away from the Sundial were still safe.

While Farah was asleep, Layla wandered Alshams in search of the mouse that had entered the city, sharing the view with her Moonchild. As a result, Farah was rather tired in the mornings.

By their third practice, everyone was almost ready to leave: homes had been packed up, and people were ready to evacuate at the final sunrise.

Farah had obsessively practised her notes. She knew them well, but she hadn't perfected the moon-magic side of the instrument: her emotions.

When Farah thought about herself, her parents' words echoed in her mind: she was dangerous, someone that needed to be kept away from others. She couldn't think of herself without this intruding on her thoughts. And that's when she would give up.

After that, all her worries spilled out of her mind like marbles dropped down a long corridor, and it would take her hours to gather them all up again.

The city was quiet when Farah snuck out to find Amira, just as the sun was about to rise for the first time since she entered Alshams. Farah knew Shurooq and Hamad wanted her to stay down here, but she had waited through the long night to see Amira, and she couldn't leave her friend to fend for herself in the desert any longer. Farah would be up and back before anyone noticed. Or so she hoped.

Farah opened the door from her bedroom slowly so it didn't creak. Layla nuzzled into her hair for comfort, and she crept through the living room and into the foyer without making a sound. Sneaking around was one of Farah's skills, and she was glad to have it now.

The coin hummed in her pocket as she crossed the bridge of Alshams towards the houses beyond. Their windows blinked at her, and she could *feel* people's dreams and nightmares drift out of the doors and wrap themselves around her.

The jellyfish glowed bright, rising to the surface as she passed above them, scuttling quietly towards the gate. Farah stepped on to the platform, not entirely sure how to work it on her own. Eventually she found a lever and pulled it, hoping.

Immediately the ground beneath her shifted. Farah's stomach flipped as the lift rose slowly, higher and higher, and Alshams shrank beneath her.

Back in the tunnel, past the golden gate, everything was dark. At the end stood an archway Farah hadn't seen before, leading to a set of stairs. It must be the route to the building above, the one that led to the desert. Layla was acting strange, clinging firm in Farah's hair, scuttling down to her shoulders, placing her clawed feet on Farah's cheeks. The closer Farah moved towards the door, the more skittish Layla became.

'We *have* to,' explained Farah, picking her *jinni* up and tucking her back in her hair nest. 'We can't leave Amira alone. We –'

Farah stopped short as she saw a pair of eyes watching her silently from the shadows. The smell of stewing apples filled the tunnel, and the creature stepped forward slowly. Farah could see the light haloed around it, just like the other *jinn*.

A deer.

Farah had now crossed paths with three of the five *jinn* they had released. And now was her chance to bind it, to put into practice everything Hamad had taught her. She reached into her pouch – but found it empty, apart from the coin.

'No!' Farah gasped into the silence. In her haste to find Amira, she had forgotten the flute.

The deer darted past her, through the golden gate to the city below. Farah chased after it for a few steps, but knew it was no use. She couldn't catch up with it now, and she didn't have the flute to bind it. Anyway, Amira was more important. Without her friend, what was the point?

As Farah jogged back towards the archway, towards her friend, a great crack tore through the wall. Part of the ceiling collapsed to the floor around her, like a crumbling cake. Farah jumped back to escape the debris and dust.

Farah caught her breath and checked on her *jinni*. Layla was OK, just a little scared. As Farah peered into the gloom, she saw a mouse dart into the rubble. And through a hole in the ceiling, stretching wide like a gaping wound, she heard the *crunch, crunch, crunch* of rock sliding beneath scales, and a hiss that grew louder as the moments passed.

Farah slumped. If she found Amira now, she would be leading the rogue *jinn* straight to her . . . and without the flute, she wouldn't be able to keep Amira safe by binding the *jinn*. So Farah returned to the Sundial, all the while sensing she was being followed through the just-waking city.

Chapter 23

'I can't do it!' Farah declared angrily, waving the flute at Hamad some hours later.

She had lied and said Layla had found the *jinn* and rubble while scouting the city, and that the lizard *jinni* had seen three others enter the city. It felt important to share the updates with Hamad, but she hadn't wanted to worry him by saying she had planned to sneak out. Shurooq and her team were now clearing the exit, and keeping watch for the snake.

Meanwhile, Hamad had sent Manayer up to search for Amira. Farah was too distracted waiting for news on her friend to think of a time when she had been mischievous.

'It would help if you could ease your worries a little,' said Hamad. 'They're clouding your judgement.'

Farah scowled, some of Amira's fire sparking inside of her. 'Are you telling me to calm down?'

Layla scuttled down to the end of the flute Farah was

holding aloft, and stuck out her forked tongue at Hamad.

'No, of course not,' Hamad said, flustered.

Farah narrowed her eyes. If going on adventures with Amira had taught her anything, it was that feeling emotion was good. Wasn't that why Farah was the one to use the flute in the first place? Because she could feel a variety of emotions?

So no, Farah wasn't going to calm down. She was going to feel, but she was going to *channel* those feelings. That's what she needed to do to save Alshams.

An awkward silence followed. Farah could sense that Hamad was holding something inside. A longing he didn't share. Amira's scents were pungent, fresh; Hamad's were more like an empty bottle of perfume, or a drawer that had once held fragrant soap. You could smell the essence of what had once been there, but you couldn't quite find it.

'You need a break,' Hamad said at last.

'I can't!' Farah replied through gritted teeth, cursing herself for forgetting her flute earlier. She'd lost her chance at finding Amira and binding the rogue *jinn* all in a single moment.

'You need to clear your head, have some distance,' Hamad said. 'You know the notes you have to play. If you keep trying like this, you'll only get more frustrated.'

Farah sulkily agreed. 'I guess,' she said. At least outside in the city, they would have more of a chance at finding the rogue *jinn*. 'Where will we go?'

Hamad grinned. 'One place that's sure to cheer you up.'

Farah put the flute away in her pocket, and Layla returned to her nest of hair.

Hamad led Farah into the foyer, where they steered themselves around newly crumbled pieces of marble, and on to the steps outside the Sundial.

In a few short hours, the houses across the river had transformed. Up ahead, beyond the bridge, were rows of brightly coloured stalls, with half of Alshams perusing them.

'What is it?' asked Farah, staring.

'The midday souk,' explained Hamad.

Farah thought back to the midnight souk, where she had met Amira and Leo. It was where they'd started their adventure to the city of brass, sailing on the back of a stolen dhow. Could this souk be the start of something, too?

'It's a long-standing tradition of moon and sun magic,' explained Hamad as they crossed the bridge. Farah peeked down at the jellyfish. No matter how many times she saw them, they would never be any less beautiful. 'Magic is all about trading and sharing.'

'So what sort of thing do people trade here?' Farah asked.

'You'll see,' said Hamad, grabbing Farah's hand as they dived into the crowd.

It was a hotpot of smells: fear mingled with resignation and worry and, beneath that, nostalgia. The people of Alshams had no real idea whether they would remain here for much longer, and so they were trying to make the most of it.

After a while, Farah was able to block out the smells, and focus on the things Hamad was showing her. Maybe her mind really was clearing. Layla bravely scuttled down her leg and darted into the crowd like an arrow. She seemed to enjoy hunting down here.

At the souk there were clothes much like the white and

gold-threaded outfits Hamad and Shurooq wore, and shoes made of silk.

'Amira would love these,' Farah said, pointing at a purple and gold pair.

'Why don't you get them for her?' Hamad suggested.

Farah had no coins to offer, apart from the special coin hidden in her pocket. When she was alone, she would twist it round her fingers, as she recalled the story Shurooq had told her. If one wish had cursed the city, could another fix it?

When the vendor recognized Farah as a Moonchild, she let her have the slippers for free.

Hamad laughed. 'That *never* happens to me, even when I show Manayer off.'

Farah grinned, and held the beaded slippers tightly. It was nice to feel as if her magic was cause for joy, rather than suspicion.

'What about the rest of your family?' she asked while they sifted through trinkets that were said to help with concentration, and cubed contraptions that unlocked the answers you were searching for if you cracked their puzzle. 'Where are your parents?'

'They're Sunseekers,' Hamad said. 'They haven't been back for a few months.'

'That must be hard,' Farah said with a frown, thinking of her sister Dalal.

Hamad shrugged. 'It's fine,' he said, although Farah could tell it wasn't. 'My older brother is with them, so I know they're OK. And I have Shurooq. I made her a promise . . .'

His sentence faded out and he brushed the back of his head awkwardly, like he didn't know what else to say.

'Can I ask you something else?' Farah said.

A group of children scuttled past, shrieking. For a moment Hamad looked as if he would say no. But then he nodded.

'How did it feel, being left behind by your brother?' Farah asked.

Hamad frowned. 'I don't really think about it. I know he has to do it, and I have to stay here. It's just how it is.'

Farah was so used to thinking about things from all angles that it had never crossed her mind that some people only thought about things once. That some people were just . . . different.

As they reached one end of the stall, Layla scuttled towards Farah, a dead beetle in her mouth. She climbed up Farah's legs, and rested on her shoulder, facing Hamad. Then she leaned forward, the bug still in her mouth.

'What is she doing?' asked Hamad a little nervously.

'She hunted for you,' said Farah, gleeful. 'That means she likes you!'

A few people in the crowd tutted at them as they stood there, blocking the path.

'Well?' said Farah. 'Aren't you going to accept it?'

Hamad looked a little queasy. 'Do I have to?'

Layla was standing on two legs now, as if she were about to launch herself at Hamad. He sighed, looking like he was about to heave, and held out his palm.

'Thank you,' he croaked at Layla, who dropped the beetle in his hands and scuttled up into Farah's hair once more.

'Go on,' said Farah.

'What?' said Hamad, fear in his eyes.

'Eat it!' said Farah. 'Or Layla will be upset.' She was joking, but she wanted to see how far she could push Hamad. Maybe she *could* be in touch with her mischievous side after all.

But before he could oblige, something tugged the slippers out of Farah's hand. She looked down to see a little mouse scuttle away with them.

'Come on!' Farah cried. 'We can't lose it!'

The crowd parted ways as Farah and Hamad sprinted after the mouse, away from the stalls and into the dark caverns that surrounded Alshams. Farah was determined not to lose the *jinni* this time. Whispers followed them like the hissing of the snake in the tunnel. She ignored them.

It was time for her to bind her first *jinni*.

Chapter 24

Layla leaped from Farah's head like a bird in flight, and landed on the tiny rogue *jinni*'s furry back. It dropped the slippers at once. Layla grabbed them, scuttling up Farah's leg with her prize.

'Farah!' Hamad called, reaching her side.

Together, they cornered the mouse *jinni*, but Farah knew it would escape unless she could bind it.

'You can do this,' Hamad urged. 'Think about what we practised.'

Farah pulled the flute from her pocket and wrapped her lips around the brass mouthpiece. She closed her eyes and thought back to the souk, moments ago, when she'd told Hamad to eat the bug. And while she did, she breathed out, hoping to hear the notes she was desperately trying to play.

But they didn't come.

Farah opened her eyes and growled in frustration as

the mouse tried to dart away through their legs. She knew she needed to dig deeper.

'Come on, Farah,' said Hamad.

'But I'm not the mischievous one,' said Farah, breathing in some of Hamad's calmness, trying to find enough to help her concentrate. 'It's Dalal –'

Farah's eyes widened as a memory floated into her mind like a stray petal from a flower. She pulled out the flute and closed her eyes, her fingers finding the notes, each one memorized to perfection.

Dalal was just a baby, crying. Farah's parents were sitting with her in the living room, as Farah listened by the stairs. Dalal's voice rose and fell, and Farah could smell her parents' frustration as they tried and failed to calm her little sister down.

'What's wrong with her?' Baba asked desperately, bouncing Dalal up and down on his lap. Mama tried to feed her, but all the while, Dalal cried, turning her face away from their offerings.

Farah knew what was wrong with her sister. She could smell it. Dalal was feeling uncomfortable and hot.

She got up and walked into the living room with Layla

on her shoulder. She was just five years old herself, but wanted desperately to help.

'Farah, go to bed,' Baba said dismissively before she had the chance to say a word. Her parents were starting to worry about Farah and her magic.

Mama walked to the door and closed it, shutting Farah out. Farah scuttled back upstairs like a lone mouse. Downstairs all she could hear was Dalal crying. She could feel her sister's discomfort like an itch. So she came up with a plan.

Farah watched from the top of the stairs as Layla scaled the walls into the kitchen. It was only another second before she heard the crash. The little lizard fled before Farah's parents saw her.

Mama went in first. Just as Farah had hoped, she called for Baba. The cupboards, it seemed, had crashed to the floor of their own accord.

Farah watched through the open door as Baba placed a crying Dalal in her cot and hurried to the kitchen. The moment he had rounded the corner, Farah leaped inside and folded her sister into her arms.

'Hush,' said Farah, one eye on the living-room door.

Dalal cried until she saw Layla peep out of Farah's hair and stick her tongue out. Then, she let out a squeal of delight. Farah quickly adjusted Dalal's clothes until she could tell they were comfortable, and gave her a kiss on the head, taking in her powdery scent, before rushing back upstairs.

Farah's parents didn't realize at first that Dalal had stopped crying when they returned to the living room. They were too busy bickering about whose job it was to clean up the mess. But when they saw their baby sound asleep, they congratulated themselves on doing such a good job as parents. Farah didn't feel *all* that bad about them having to spend most of the night cleaning up the remains of their kitchen.

As Farah thought back to that moment, she started to hear the notes emerge from the flute. Almost at once, the mouse was entranced. It stood up on tiptoe and swayed to and fro. When the song was done, the mouse was still. Then, very suddenly, it scuttled up Farah's arm and rested on her shoulder. Layla peered over her nest, seeming rather unamused.

Farah squealed.

'You did it!' Hamad laughed in delight. 'What did you
think about?'

Farah paused, not wanting to share. But she knew that holding it inside would only make things worse. 'My sister,' she finally said.

Hamad widened his eyes. 'That's it! That's the key. Your sister must be the one who brings out the most emotion in you. You need to think of a memory involving your sister each time.'

'Yes, but –'

'*That* is how you'll be able bind all the *jinn*,' Hamad said with certainty.

Farah fell silent. The truth was, she had tried very hard *not* to think about her sister. It hurt too much. But maybe Hamad was right. If they had any chance at saving Alshams, Farah had to face her own emotions.

As they walked back to the Sundial, Farah side-eyed the mouse on her shoulder. 'You're the reason we've been separated from Amira,' she muttered, thinking back to her last time in the desert, and how the mouse had dragged her away from Amira. The mouse twitched its tiny nose as if to apologize.

Layla stuck her forked tongue out at the mouse and retreated into her nest, turning her tail on the *jinni* as if to make a point.

'I should check on Manayer,' Hamad said, pulling his goggles down. 'She'll have seen something by now.'

His shoulders slumped.

'What's wrong?' Farah asked, smelling his concern almost at once. 'What do you see?'

Hamad pulled the goggles up so they sat on top of his head and looked at Farah with a pained expression on his face. 'Don't freak out,' he began.

Which, of course, worried Farah even more. 'What is it? Has Manayer seen something?'

'Yes . . .' said Hamad. 'And no. I guess that's the point . . .'

'Spit it out!'

'Amira's gone,' Hamad finally said. 'So is Namur. Manayer can't . . . she can't find them anywhere.'

Chapter 25

Hello again. How have you been? It's been a bumpy journey so far, don't you agree? Although I'm afraid it's about to get bumpier.

Before I catch you up, did you guess correctly? I gave you three options for what happened next. Did you guess the second one? Or did you think Amira and I would be reunited?

Well done if you got it right. This time, I want you to try and imagine how this will end. It'll be your story after this, so you must practise. Especially as I'm not sure whether I'll be around to tell it for much longer.

With only one sunrise left after this one, Hamad and I have just three of the eight *jinn* on our side. There's the snake, still out there of course, and the deer roaming around Alshams. And there's Semek and Namur, wherever they've both gone. And what about the final *jinn*? I can't

seem to remember it. If you think back to Alhitan, and the *jinn* released from their bottles, you might be able to help me out.

I must go. I have a lot more *jinn* hunting to do. I know Hamad said not to call it that, but I'm sure the *jinn* won't mind.

If you don't hear from me again, that means I've failed my mission. But for now, goodbye, and wish us luck on the last leg of our journey.

Chapter 26

Later, as the final long night arrived, Farah, Layla and the mouse were sitting alone in her room.

Farah had banished the mouse to a corner, where she had placed a cushion and a slice of cheese. Just because she had bound it, didn't mean she had got over its attempt to kidnap Layla. And it was still a little too mischievous for her liking. It had a habit of nibbling at the corners of the cushion, so very quickly the feathers began to seep out like the blood on her wound. And it liked to run up and down her legs at great speed.

Farah tried to picture the human who would eventually pair with the mouse *jinni*. They would be mischievous, like Dalal, always playing pranks. But deep down, there would be a part of them that was sweet too.

Farah pulled the coin from her pocket and examined it again. Layla had brought it to her for a reason. Did she want Farah to make a wish? So far, they only knew the location of three of the *jinn*, and Amira had disappeared from their camp in the desert. But why? Why had she chosen to leave Farah?

Worms crawled in Farah's belly when she thought of it. Was Amira mad because Farah had abandoned her? Or was she secretly pleased to be rid of her? And then there was the worst thought of all: what if something terrible had happened to Amira?

That's when Farah knew what she had to do. If all the *jinn* didn't arrive in time to save Alshams, she would *wish* for them to come instead, at the risk of losing something greater. Would that be Layla, or her sister Dalal? Neither bore thinking about. So, as usual, Farah shoved her worries aside and tried to fall asleep. Except when you try *not* to think of something really hard, you just end up thinking about it even more instead.

Only when Farah's breathing had found a rhythm, and her light snores filled the silence of the room, did Layla crawl from her hair nest and out of the window to explore the city.

That night, Farah's dreams took a more whimsical turn.

Layla scuttled along the quiet city in the dark, the golden spires shining down on them, carrying with them the remaining light from the sun. She could hear her *jinni*'s heart beating in time with her steps. From some unseen source came a silver light that reminded Farah of the moon. It was different to the gold that shone through the city during the day.

Layla took her to the heart of the city, to a small patch of grassland that stood behind the school. And standing in the middle of the grass, head bent in search of food, was the deer. The rogue *jinni* she had seen in the tunnel.

Farah somehow willed herself awake before Layla could return. The mouse was asleep in its corner, and she crept quietly across the room so as not to wake it. She didn't want mischief to follow her tonight.

Farah didn't stop to wake Hamad. She didn't even stop to put her shoes on. She just grabbed the flute and ran out of the door, her bare feet slamming against the cool floor of the city as she retraced Layla's steps towards the school, her heart picking up pace.

Layla met her at the corner of the school, scuttling up to her shoulder. The deer looked up at Farah startled, and ran a few paces away. It was acting as it had in the tunnel. Skittish.

Farah frowned. She had to get close enough to catch its scent, to know what its emotion was. But each time she took a step, so did the deer. It watched her, eyes pricked, and for a long time they danced to and fro.

Farah decided to sit, legs folded beneath her, on the grass.

The deer stopped edging away, but didn't come any closer.

Farah tried her best to seem calm, so as not to startle it again. Perhaps she should have fetched Hamad after all. He would be better with an animal like this one. Or he would calm her enough to play the flute.

Farah sat, twirling the flute between her fingers. Her eyes were beginning to droop, and she worried she would fall asleep and miss her chance. The feeling reminded her of the long nights she would sit on her windowsill while her parents threw their parties far below. She would sit, patiently, and wait until everyone was asleep and she could escape into the desert for a moment of freedom.

She knew it was time to go whenever she heard Dalal

sneak into her room, her feet pitter-pattering on the cold floor.

'Ready?' Dalal would say, grinning up at Farah with a crooked smile.

The flute began to hum in Farah's hands, where moments before it had been still. Farah lifted it to her lips and played a note. It was softer than when she had played for the mouse, but it was there.

Farah played the notes rhythmically, welcoming the *jinni* into her fold.

Slowly, the deer approached, and she could finally smell its emotion through Layla.

Patience.

Chapter 27

The Sundial had turned into a menagerie, with a lizard, a falcon, a mouse and a deer now roaming around. Over the final long night, they each settled into their own spaces in Shurooq's apartments.

The mouse preferred the kitchen, nibbling at the food and gnawing at the table leg. Farah made sure to keep the slippers she had bought Amira well away from its little teeth. The deer spent most of her time in Farah's room. Layla, of course, did her best to remind the others that she was Farah's true *jinni*, and sat regally on Farah's head like a crown.

The snake was out there, Farah knew it was. Lurking. Waiting. But for what?

All they could do now was wait for the final sunrise, and hope somehow they would gather the rest of the *jinn* before the sun rays ran out. When Farah had arrived at Alshams, the fireball had been the size of a house. It had shrunk to the size of a horse, and resembled a chair now, barely visible to the city beyond.

The golden glow had faded further, and even the neon fish seemed less luminous. The colour of Alshams was vanishing, along with the hope of its people. Their worries weighed Farah down, and each hour felt more difficult than the last.

Hamad had checked on Manayer a few times, though she'd still seen no sign of Amira.

'She really just . . . disappeared?' said Farah. There was a dull ache in her heart whenever she thought of her friend. The uncertainty was the worst part. Was this how she'd made Dalal feel?

Hamad frowned. 'I know it sounds impossible, but there are no tracks left at the camp. It's almost as if she was snatched.'

Farah bit her lip. Rocs didn't fly this far into the desert, did they? And if Amira had been snatched, why would all of her things be gone, too? No. It was clear to Farah that Amira had chosen to leave. But why? Wasn't Amira the one who had been so determined to save everyone in Alshams? Farah didn't know whether to be sad or angry, so she settled for a mixture of both.

'I'm sorry,' said Hamad. 'Snatched was the wrong word to use. I mean . . .'

'I know,' Farah sighed. 'I just don't understand it.'

'Neither do I,' said Hamad.

For the first time, Farah could sense his fear that just maybe, they wouldn't succeed. It wrapped around her like a blanket, and swirled round and round her head like a sandstorm, clogging her thoughts. And after a while, she couldn't see through the dust at all.

As the final sunrise approached, Farah became skittish.

She fiddled with the coin in her pocket, imagining the moment she would have to pull it out.

The city was emptying, slowly, like ants marching from their hills carrying their lives on their backs. They would head for the desert. And then what? Would they be forced to camp and move around, like Farah's nomadic ancestors? Would magic just be a memory, a legend in their lives?

Farah hadn't seen Shurooq or Hamad for some time. They were busy helping everyone leave while Farah watched for the final *jinn*, still hoping Amira would return. She imagined the Sundial years from now: a relic some adventurer would stumble on, its story lost to the world. Except if Alshams didn't survive, nothing else would either. The weight of responsibility bore down on Farah's shoulders like the weight of Alhitan on the whale's back. She couldn't let it happen. She wouldn't. She would use the coin if she had to.

The day wore on, until Hamad returned to the foyer.

'We don't have the *jinn*,' Farah said by way of greeting. 'This sunrise is only set to last another hour. Once it's gone, we're stuck. That's it. And after that . . .'

'The *jinn* will come,' Hamad said, his face taut.

'No they won't!' Farah growled, her voice reverberated round the Sundial louder than she had expected. She echoed Amira's words from the desert. 'Good things don't always happen to good people.'

'What's that supposed to mean?' Hamad said. 'We *have* to keep fighting. If we don't we've already lost.' He sounded so calm; so infuriatingly calm.

'You know what you are?' Farah finally spat. 'You're like sand! Mouldable. You don't have your own path. You just shape yourself to every situation. You let water sweep over you, the wind carry you away –'

'Sand also puts out fire,' Hamad reminded her.

'THAT IS NOT THE POINT,' Farah exploded. Her fear had been slowly building. Now, with no other options left, she felt completely out of control. With her fists clenched, she stormed out of the front door of the Sundial and ran to the river with its jellyfish.

Hamad jogged after her, stopping a few metres behind.

From her pocket, Farah pulled out the coin. She had to do it now or it would be too late. She held it in her palm, closed her eyes, and took a breath, envisaging her wish. Alshams would be restored, in the sun. Everyone – including Amira and Dalal – would be safe and happy.

'Farah, wait!' Hamad called, his voice urgent.

Farah wrapped her hand around the coin as he approached, holding it behind her back and turning away from the lake. 'I'm sick of waiting,' she said, Layla clinging to her hair. 'Look where it's got us! I should've gone back out. Searched for her. I should've tried to find the *jinn* instead of just sitting there and hoping they'd arrive. I –'

'No, Farah, you don't understand,' said Hamad. To her surprise he was smiling.

'What?' Farah said, not caring. 'What could you

possibly be grinning about?'

'They're almost here!'

Hamad's excitement bubbled up inside Farah, making her feel giddy. 'Who?'

'Your friend Amira, and the missing Moonchild . . . Leo.'

From behind her back, Farah dropped the coin, relieved she didn't have to make her wish. She turned to watch it sink, sink, sink to the depths of the river once more.

Chapter 28

Farah sprinted across the city, over the bridge and into the crowd shuffling towards the platform to take them up to the desert. She weaved in and out, and jostled her way on to the platform just as it started to move. 'Sorry!' she said to the people around her, anxiously searching for Hamad. 'I have to get through . . .'

'Farah!' Hamad screamed from the crowd, his head bobbing up and down. 'Wait!'

'Hamad!' Farah called, reaching for him. Their fingers grazed, but the platform was too quick, and his hand slipped from hers.

'I'll catch the next one, Farah. Don't -'

His words were cut short by a baby who had started to cry, and Hamad was swallowed into the crowd once more.

As soon as the platform stopped, Farah hurled herself off and through the open archway at the end of the tunnel. The crack still stood like a warning, but the crowds were too loud for Farah to listen for the snake. Groups of people were dragging their luggage up a long set of stairs that seemed to go on and on forever. Farah joined them.

At the very top, Farah wearily entered the building – the one that had collapsed into dust so many times before – and opened the front door. The heat of the desert hit her like a wave, and the sandstorm that surrounded the building pulled at her clothes.

The sun blinded Farah as she stumbled out into the sands, while others pushed behind her. She held her hands above her eyes, trying to spot Amira and Leo through the crowd while she found a spot that was free of twirling sand.

Farah could smell her before she saw her. Fire, burning strong. Leo too, his scent like oranges. And then suddenly she was on the floor as Amira slammed into her for a fierce hug.

'You're OK!' Amira said, tears streaming down her face. She looked between Leo and Farah and declared, 'Neither of you are allowed to leave me, ever again.'

Leo looked surprisingly well, given that he had been snatched by the stormbird and taken to the horizon. He grinned at Farah. They hugged a little more gently.

Hamad finally caught up. Farah introduced them all before her eyes returned to Amira and Leo. Namur was, as Amira explained, perched invisible around her neck, while Semek swam around a jar of water in Leo's arms, a permanent look of surprise on his face.

'Where have you been?' said Farah. 'Both of you?' Her eyes landed on a fox, nuzzling up against Amira's leg. 'And who's the fox?'

Amira waved the fox away as if it were a fly. 'Ignore her,

she's very annoying.'

'Is she a *jinni*?' asked Hamad.

Amira rolled her eyes. 'Yes. And she won't leave me alone.'

Farah could smell the fox now: warm, inviting, like honey bread. She glanced at Hamad.

'That's seven,' Hamad said. 'Once Manayer returns.'

'We're close,' Farah said, hope fizzing through her veins.

Amira waved her hands between the two of them. 'Remember us? Your friends? We haven't seen each other in a while. Stop muttering to each other and tell us what's going on.'

Farah hurried through, explaining that they had to gather all the *jinn* and return to Alshams together before the sun set.

'We'll go down as soon as this crowd has cleared and Manayer is back from scouting. She'll soon realize we're all together,' Hamad said. 'It's important everyone in the city gets out safely first. After the sun sets today, the entrance will be locked forever. At least, until we restore the city.'

'What about the final *jinni*?' asked Leo.

'Is it the snake?' said Amira. Resentment, like hard-boiled eggs, seeped out of her.

Farah nodded. 'Have you seen it since I left?'

Amira shook her head. 'No. Only the fox. But my, you won't *believe* the adventure I've been on.'

And, without pausing, she launched into her story.

The Sea Witch, Her Cat Jinni and the Longest Night

The sea witch woke just before the sun set to find the Moonchild and her lizard *jinni* had gone. All that remained was a house in the distance, surrounded by date trees. And twisting round the trees was a sandstorm.

The sea witch was used to storms out at sea – waves crashing, threatening to drag her under – but she wasn't accustomed to the desert. Was her friend trapped inside the building? Had she been injured in the storm? What other secrets did the desert hold?

As the sea witch searched for her friend, the sandstorm reached for her, like a giant hand carved from dust. The sand moved in waves, making the ground rumble, and seemed to expand as she approached.

But the sea witch was determined. She wouldn't abandon her friend! And so she pushed against the storm as it twisted her round and round, tangling her hair and clothes. She was just about to reach the house, to go inside, her hand wrapped around the handle of the door. But just as she grasped it, it crumbled to pieces.

A cloud of dust threw the sea witch and her *jinni* back. She fell to the ground coughing and spluttering. When she looked up again, the sandstorm was gone. So too was the building.

The sea witch returned to her camp, with no sign of her friend. She peered at her map – to see that the city they were searching for stood just where the house had appeared. And she sensed a strange lingering magic: a magic born out of sand and wind.

The sea witch hoped, desperately, that her friend was safe, and she planned to wait for her until the next sunrise.

As the long night wore on the sea witch lit her bakhoor pot and told her *jinni* stories until she fell asleep, the smoke wrapping around them both to keep them safe and warm.

When the sea witch woke it was still dark. Up above, the sky had turned a haze of blue-green light. And, just as she had glimpsed on the dhow, the light moved, reshaping the stars so they formed the shapes of eight *jinn*: the very same *jinn* the sea witch and her friends had released from their bottles on the island of brass. And she knew moon magic was at its strongest.

The sea witch watched the sky, alive, entranced. Stars danced around the moon, circling it in celebration, dancing faster and faster until they made her dizzy.

As the long night wore on, the sea witch grew hungry. She no longer had the energy for stories, but she kept her bakhoor pot lit, allowing the fire to heat her and her *jinni*. She had planned, at first, to wait until the next sunrise, when she hoped the strange building would return, and she could go after her friend. But as she read the pages of the notebook she had inherited, she found a new path. One set by the very first Moonchild she had met, the boy who had been taken to the horizon.

On one page the boy had drawn the eight *jinn* together in a circle, just as they had appeared on the table at Alhitan; just as they appeared in the sky now. And right in the middle of the table, was the sun.

The boy had understood that the moon and sun must be balanced in order for the earth to keep spinning.

It was, he wrote, a basic fact of science.

When the sea witch turned the page, she saw a note, barely legible, scribbled on the other side: *Horizon = Jinn realm?*

She knew, then, that the boy wasn't gone for good. He had been taken to the *jinn* realm.

And so, with her cat *jinni* on her shoulders, her fists clenched in determination, the sea witch let the smoke of her bakhoor pot wrap around her body, and then she told a new story.

'Once, in the desert, a sea witch and her cat *jinni* went in search of the *jinn* realm.'

The smoke formed, and took the shape of the sea witch and her *jinni* walking through the desert. The smoke sea witch held out her arm, the one that bore her father's ring, and she drew an arch in the air in front of her, which turned into a door.

The sea witch paused, studying the ring on her own, real hand, glowing green in the dark. She did the same as her smoke counterpart, and watched as a silver platform rose from the ground before her. Three steps led up to a pillared arch, with mirrored doors coated in silver and brass.

Carrying her bakhoor pot, the sea witch tentatively took the steps, and opened the door.

Walking into the *jinn* realm was like dancing through the night sky. Silver stars sparkled all around and, wherever you turned, the moon shone big and bright, more beautiful than she had ever seen.

The sea witch walked along a starlit beach, shining waves lapping at the shore in a gentle rhythm. The ocean glowed with thousands of creatures, luminous and full of colour. She was so distracted that she forgot to continue her story. She turned to her smoke counterpart, who was standing, waiting for instruction, and she cleared her throat.

'The sea witch and her *jinni* searched for their friend along a starlit beach, as the moon watched over them for protection.'

Up ahead the stars moved, taking shape of the different *jinn*.

The smoke sea witch changed direction, turning right. Ahead the real sea witch saw, floating in front of her as if swimming through the ocean, a golden fish.

The fish swam through the air, and the sea witch chased it.

'Stop!' she called. 'Please, stop!'

She tripped and fell hard on the ground. But a warm hand reached for her, helping her up, and she found herself face to face with her very first friend.

'It's you!' said the sea witch pulling her lost friend close. 'How? How are you here?'

He looked well, his face glowing. And as they settled down on the beach with the waves lapping at their feet, he told his story.

'I'll begin,' he said, 'where you last saw me.'

The Moonchild, the Stormbird and the Journey to the Horizon

The Moonchild was on the island of Alhitan, just as it was sinking and the stormbird was attacking, when he understood what needed to happen. In order to defeat the monster, he had to let it take him to the horizon, just as the story at Alhitan had told.

Being versed in science, the Moonchild suspected what would meet him at the horizon: the *jinn* realm. And in exchange for his sacrifice, the Sahar Peninsula would be safe.

The Moonchild hoped his friends would find a way to free him. It was a risk, but he trusted them. And so he left his notebook behind, and let himself be swept up and carried to the horizon.

As the Moonchild had suspected, the stormbird's nest stood in the crack between the worlds. The great monster took him there, ready to devour him whole. Quickly, he opened his bag and laid out eight bottles of brass, one by one.

The stormbird let out a cry of rage as the bottles pulled it in, shrinking away like a dying fire. Its eyes, beak, head, claws, wings and body split into eight pieces, each representing a different emotion, and vanished into the bottles – until all that remained was a single giant feather.

And finally, after days and weeks of chaos, all was still.

The Moonchild gathered up the bottles of brass. To make sure the stormbird wouldn't return, he stepped into the *jinn* realm on the far side of the great nest to hide them: a world of darkness and stars, and animals made of moondust.

And there, he waited for his friends to find him, knowing they would someday be reunited.

Chapter 29

'Time is strange in the *jinn* realm,' Leo explained. 'It felt as if only a few days had passed before Amira found me.'

The final sunset arrived by the time Leo and Amira had finished their stories. Manayer had just landed on Hamad's arm, a package tied to her feet.

'When I was there,' Leo continued, 'I made friends with a moondust fox. It was one of the *jinni* we released from the bottles. It stayed with me and Semek. And then, when Amira came to free us, it followed us into the world.'

Farah glanced at the fox now. She finally recognized its scent: loyalty.

'So that leaves the snake?' said Farah. 'And then we have them all?'

Amira cleared her throat. 'I hate to rush you, but the sun is setting *really* quickly.'

There was only a glimpse of the sun left. The moon was

already rising, waiting to take over for good. The sandstorm reached its full height, trying to push them away. And, as she had many times before in the desert, Farah ran. The other Moonchildren followed.

Every inhabitant of Alshams stood out in the desert now, and their eyes followed the children as they swam against the current. Farah burst through the door of the house just as the building began to collapse. The ground pulled the four Moonchildren and five *jinn* down to the city of Alshams. Farah's stomach leaped as the sand swallowed them up – and the group fell down, down, down, a pile of flailing limbs.

Farah heard it before she saw it. The soft hiss that made her blood run cold, and the back of her neck tingle. Tucked away at the back of the tunnel, curled up in the shadows, was the snake. The last rogue *jinni*. It smelled like ash, just as it had in the desert. And Farah understood its emotion now.

Fear.

It was time for Farah to face it. To admit her biggest fear to herself.

Chapter 30

The snake hissed, lashing out at Farah, almost biting her neck before Hamad dragged her back.

Amira lit the bakhoor pot and started weaving a story together, while Leo and the fox sent dust into the tunnel with the help of Namur and Manayer, confusing the beast.

Layla tucked herself into Farah's nest of hair, comforting her like always, while Hamad stood by her side so she could absorb his calmness and clear her mind.

Farah understood now that the snake was acting out, just as she had when she thought their plan had failed. It wasn't causing fear. It was afraid.

The smoke from Amira's bakhoor pot surrounded them like a protective cloak. Farah closed her eyes and listed her fears, whispering them so only Hamad could hear.

I'm afraid my parents are ashamed of me.

I'm afraid everyone thinks I'm weird.

I'm afraid I'm different.

I'm afraid I'm cursed.

Farah placed her trembling lips and shaking hands around the flute. But no sound came out.

'Dig deeper, Farah,' said Hamad, as if he could read her thoughts.

Farah shook her head and opened her eyes again. She couldn't.

The snake had the fox *jinni* in its clutches now, wrapped around its body as if it would squeeze the life out of it. Namur and Manayer tried desperately to free the fox, but the snake was faster, stronger – growing with Farah's fears.

Amira's smoke blanket turned into a horse, but her magic was failing too, and the horse turned into a puff of smoke before it could reach the snake.

The fox whimpered.

Namur hissed.

Manayer let out a cry.

And the snake watched Farah, triumphant.

Hamad squeezed Farah's shoulder. Layla nuzzled into

her hair. Farah closed her eyes and remembered the time when her worst fear had come true. She had felt, in that moment, as if all her hope was lost. It was how she was feeling now, as she watched the snake win.

On the night Farah had run away from home, she had waited for her parents to fall asleep so she and Dalal could explore together.

She had stepped into the hallway, intending to brush her teeth, when she heard them. It was a bit late for her parents to have guests, so she scuttled silently down the stairs and listened.

'Now?' said her mother. 'It's late. She'll be asleep. Can't it wait until tomorrow?'

'No,' said her father. 'This has been going on long enough.'

Her mother sighed. 'What will you do?'

A man whose voice Farah didn't recognize spoke. 'We'll use brass. Trap the *jinni*, until we can find a way to destroy her. The magic will be gone then.'

'Just like that?' asked her father.

'Yes,' said the man. 'Like plucking a weed from a bed of flowers.'

'And it'll save us the embarrassment once and for all,' her father muttered.

Farah's blood ran cold. They were planning on taking Layla away from her. Her *jinni* nuzzled into her hair, begging her not to let it happen. Farah understood now that her parents had never been concerned for her. They weren't trying to protect her. They were ashamed.

No matter how hard she tried, she would never make them understand. And so there was only one option left for her.

Farah rushed down the hall into her sister's room.

Dalal was sleeping, but woke with a yawn. 'Is it time?' she said, eyes sparkling in the moonlight.

Farah shook her head. 'Not today,' she said. 'I have to go.'

Dalal frowned. 'Where?'

Farah didn't know. She'd never been out of her village, didn't know what stood beyond the desert. 'Away,' she said eventually.

Dalal began to cry. 'I want to come with you,' she howled.

Farah glanced fearfully at her sister's bedroom door.

She could hear her parents' footsteps, and she was sure they would check on Dalal if they heard her fuss. 'You can't. I have to go. I'll find a way to contact you.'

The last thing Farah saw, as she climbed down the date tree from her sister's window, were Dalal's shining eyes. And she feared, more than anything, that she would never see her sister again. Eventually, she would just be a memory, worn down by time like weathered cliffs on the oceanside. And when Dalal grew up, she would forget that she'd once had a sister who loved her to the stars.

As Farah finished the memory, she breathed into the flute, transferring all her fears into the music. And the

song she had perfected played louder than all the times before.

Immediately, the snake stopped hissing.

Its grip on the fox loosened.

As each note twisted through the air, the snake shrank to its normal size.

With the last sunrise gone, Farah had done it. She had bound the rogue *jinn*.

There was no time to celebrate. The city of Alshams was still crumbling. They had one more task ahead of them.

'We need to get to the Sundial before the fire burns out,' cried Farah.

The tunnel began to collapse around them. Waves of sand, dust and rock chased them towards the moving platform.

The ruined city of Alshams, clinging on with its final breath, shone dimly from below.

Chapter 31

Farah led the way across the bridge, past the jellyfish and into the Sundial. The walls were collapsing around them and they had to dodge falling rocks dropping from the ceiling like shooting stars. The city had turned into a waterfall of sand, crumbling inwards, threatening to trap them for all eternity.

The hovering fireball was now as small as an apple. They didn't have much time.

The four Moonchildren and their *jinn* ran up the stairs to the centre of the Sundial, which held the last of Alshams' rays.

Shurooq was there, the deer and mouse by her side, waiting for instruction. Farah could feel her grief, like a tidal wave, as the last ray of light disappeared, leaving behind smoke and lost promise.

'No!' groaned Farah. She stared into space as if willing the spark back to life. They had come so far – and still, it wasn't enough. 'What do we do?' she asked Shurooq.

Shurooq shook her head. 'There's nothing we can do,' she said, her voice soft.

Farah's body felt like it was on fire. 'No,' she croaked again.

Hamad and Amira comforted her, wrapping her up in their shared sadness.

Leo had a frown on his face as he inspected the empty glass casing. Once it held a ball of fire the size of a house, now it was nothing but smoke. 'There *is* something we can do,' he said. 'But we have to be quick.'

No one moved.

'Do as I say, and I'll explain.' said Leo confidently.

He crouched by the base of the glass casing and placed both of his hands on the brass base. Then he waited for everyone to do the same.

'Make sure your hands are dry, and rub them against the brass,' he said as the others crouched beside him. 'The *jinn* too. They can use their fur.'

'How?' asked Farah, at the same time as Hamad and Amira.

'Static electricity,' Leo explained. 'You need something

with a positive charge – hands, fur, things like that –'
Namur started headbutting the brass, while the fox opted
for its bushy tail – 'alongside something with a negative
charge, like brass.'

'And then what?' asked Farah, feeling the warmth
beneath her hands. The friction of rubbing the brass was
starting to burn, but she didn't stop.

'The sun rays are made of gas,' Leo explained. 'The
static electricity will light it.'

'Are you sure?'

'In theory, yes. But I don't know if it'll work in pra—'

'Just say YES IT'LL WORK, Leo,' Amira snapped.
'Why is science always so long-winded with you?'

She started laughing, amused by her own anger. It was
infectious. First Hamad, then Leo and Shurooq followed.
And finally Farah. Now they were all laughing hysterically
while trying to create an electric current.

If they were going down, at least they would be smiling.

Hope suddenly sparked in the form of fire. It was
miniscule, but it was there, ready to fight.

'It worked!' screamed Farah, releasing her hands from
the brass. With the end in sight, she suddenly felt

invincible, like she could do anything.

'Now we line up the *jinn*!' said Amira. 'Just like in Alhitan.'

Leo grinned. 'Yes! I'll keep going with the charge.'

Farah smiled at her friends, glad not to do this alone. With one look from her, the rogue *jinn* surrounded the flickering flame, while the others joined at the request of their humans. The ground rumbled and quaked. And very slowly, they began to rise.

'This flame won't last for long!' warned Leo, still rubbing.

'Amira,' said Farah 'can you use your bakhoor pot to lift this faster?' And, 'Hamad,' Farah continued as Amira set to work. 'I'll take over. Send Manayer to lead us up using your goggles. Help Amira.'

Hamad stood back, pulling his goggles down. Manayer flew out of the room and into the city, circling the building as it moved up through the vast cavern towards the desert above.

'I'll go again,' said Shurooq to Leo. 'You take a break.'

Farah grinned at Shurooq as the platform lifted higher and higher. She could see relief bloom on the woman's face like flowers in spring. The houses of Alshams rose alongside them. The spires would follow, and finally the lake.

'The city,' said Shurooq, her voice full of emotion. 'It's rising like the sun.'

Smoke drifted from the bahkoor pot as Amira's story began, and a great wave of smoke filled the city like the ocean waves and sneaked into the cracks. Up, up, up they went.

'It's working,' Amira said. 'I feel so powerful!'

Farah laughed, feeling completely giddy.

'Manayer can see the sky now,' shouted Hamad. 'We're close!'

And then the sky broke through. It was unlike any sky Farah had seen before. One side of the sky was dark, the moon shining bright and full. The black and blue tones of night faded to red and pink, the bright sun at its centre.

The people of Alshams stood in the desert, watching their city rise in stunned silence. Then slowly, like a ripple, one clap followed another, and another, building up momentum. A steady rhythm picked up pace, echoing across the desert.

The claps broke into cheers that sounded like birdsong.

And from somewhere nearby, music began to play.

Chapter 32

The city celebrated. Very quickly the people gathered, cooking feast upon feast, playing music into the night to honour the moon and sun.

Amira and Leo explored the celebrations while Shurooq made sure everyone returned safely to their homes, which now stood proudly above ground. The damage to the city remained, but Farah knew it would be rebuilt bigger and stronger, now that the balance was restored.

Sitting in the main room of the Sundial, its cushions covered in dust and its tables toppled, Farah felt as if she could sleep for a thousand years. But there was one thing left to do.

She smiled at the *jinn* clustered around her. They were all here, bar Layla, Namur and Semek.

'They're free to go,' said Hamad quietly. He gazed at Manayer, and Farah now understood his worries. He was scared she would leave him. 'They're just waiting for you to release them.'

The flute's song sounded sad this time, the notes falling instead of lifting. All of the *jinn*'s emotions surged through Farah as she played: mischief, loyalty, fear and patience. She felt the emotions of the others too: anger, nerves, her own curiosity, and calmness. She fell to the floor as she bore the weight of them all.

The mouse left first, followed by the snake.

The weight eased.

The deer and fox were next.

Now Farah could stand up again.

Finally, there was Manayer.

The falcon *jinni* flew into the air and circled the room. For a moment it seemed as if she would fly out of the door. But then she landed, firm on Hamad's arm, and nipped his nose affectionately.

Hamad pulled her close. Silent tears slid down his cheeks, which he wiped on his shoulder. Farah took Layla into the kitchen to make tea, and to give Hamad and Manayer some time to themselves.

When she brought the tea back out, Hamad held a

small package in his hands.

'I didn't tell you before,' he said, 'in case nothing came of it . . . But I sent Manayer to find your sister. And she came back with this.' He held up the package. 'It's for you.'

A piece of paper was stuck to the package. Farah recognized her sister's handwriting at once.

She took a deep breath, and read the note.

The Tale of the Moonchild's Younger Sister

The Moonchild's younger sister looked up to her. She remembered when she was much smaller, and the Moonchild had looked after her. She remembered too the games they had played together, and the stories they had shared.

She loved her sister more than anything in the world.

And so, the night the Moonchild ran away, her sister wept. She wept until morning, until she was so exhausted she finally fell asleep.

After days of moping around her sister's room, playing with her old toys and trying on her clothes, the Moonchild's sister made a promise. She would, one day, go in search of her big sister. She would join her, wherever she went.

Every night, she made a wish to the moon to send her a sign that her sister thought of her. That wish was answered. Twice. Once via a note delivered by a roc, and once through the arrival of a falcon *jinni*. It tap, tap, tapped on her window, during the longest night.

'I know what you are,' the Moonchild's sister whispered, hoping her parents wouldn't hear. The falcon hopped closer to her, perching on her knee. 'I was always jealous, you know? I wanted one just like you. I wanted to be magical like her.'

'Dalal?' said a woman's voice through the door. 'Who are you talking to?'

'No one,' called the Moonchild's sister. 'That's my mother,' she said to the falcon. 'You'll have to leave. But will you give my sister this diary?'

The Moonchild's sister carefully tied her parcel to the falcon's outstretched leg, before scribbling a note. Then she watched from the window as the falcon swooped into the desert with a cry, flying, like a star, towards the moon.

Chapter 33

When Farah had finished reading the note, Hamad handed her the diary. It was filled with stories and drawings.

Dalal had been writing to Farah this whole time. She wanted to join her.

Farah took a deep breath and looked at Hamad. 'When I said you were like the sand, I didn't mean what I said. I'm sorry.'

Hamad smiled. 'Don't worry about it.'

Farah twisted her fingers round her tunic. 'I mean, you *are* like the sand, but in a good way. You bury emotions deep inside yourself, but they're still there, like hidden shells. And just look at all the things that sand can do: build houses from nothing, rise up from a buried cavern. *That's* what I should have said when I told you you're like sand.'

When Farah looked up again, Hamad was grinning. 'What about you?' he said. 'What are you like?'

Farah thought. 'I'm like the wind,' she finally said. 'Flitting from one thing to the next, carrying the weight of those around me.'

'I agree,' said Hamad. 'The wind can put out fire, but start it too. It can cause storms, but ease them. And, together with sand, it can raise buried cities from the ground.'

Farah nodded. 'I like that,' she said.

Some time later Amira and Leo burst through the doors, the noise of the city's celebrations following them inside.

'That food was *delicious*,' said Amira. 'Best I've had. Don't tell Jamila I said that.'

Farah laughed, feeling Amira's warmth enveloping them. Leo balanced her in a way Farah hadn't realized before. Leo stopped and chatted with Hamad for a bit, getting to know him, before Farah pulled Amira aside.

'I got you a present,' she said, pulling from the pouch the slippers she had found at the midday souk.

Amira's eyes lit up and she clapped her hands. 'Perfect!' she said, trying them on. 'Just perfect. Actually . . .' She looked serious now, nervous. 'I have something for you too.'

She removed her father's emerald ring from her finger, and held it out for Farah. It was identical to Shurooq's, apart from its colour.

'I can't –' Farah began.

'You can. You're the best Moonchild of us all,' insisted Amira. She grinned. 'The main character.'

Farah laughed. 'It wasn't about that, I know now. It was about us coming together.'

'Way to ruin my speech,' Amira pouted, jokingly.

Farah took the ring from her friend, and it felt oddly like they were saying goodbye. Perhaps they were.

Amira frowned. 'You won't forget about me, will you? Even if we don't see each other for a while?'

'I could never forget about you,' Farah said. '*Ever*. You'll haunt my dreams.'

'Or nightmares,' muttered Amira. 'I will miss you, you know?'

Farah felt something prickle in her chest. Before she had met Amira and Leo, she had never had any friends. Amira and the others liked her, truly, for who she was.

'I will miss you too,' said Farah, pulling Amira in for a hug.

Shurooq joined them, looking exhausted but happy. Hamad poured her a fresh cup of tea. The group huddled together, surrounded by their *jinn*.

'What are you all going to do now?' Shurooq asked.

Leo spoke first. 'I'm going to visit my mum, and we can go on our very first voyage together.'

'And you?' Shurooq said, lingering on Amira.

'I'm going to go back to *Tigerheart*,' said Amira with a

shrug. 'And then, who knows?'

Shurooq nodded. 'And you, Farah. Will you go home, too?'

Farah twisted the emerald ring, feeling the coolness of the metal, the weight of the magic inside. 'No,' she said, her eyes landing on Amira. 'I'm going to collect moondust from the *jinn* realm.'

'And *I'm* going to help,' added Hamad.

Farah looked at Hamad with surprise.

'If you'll let me?' Hamad added.

Farah narrowed her eyes. 'I'll have to think about it,' she said.

The group spent the rest of the afternoon drinking tea and eating sugary pastry sweets before piling on to the wide sofa along the wall for a well-deserved sleep. With one adventure finished, they had another approaching, as sure as the rising sun.

After all, as Jamila had always said: all great adventures begin with a nap.

Chapter 34

I always thought the rising sun was a certainty. But life is much more unexpected than we first imagine it to be.

I thought I had to be the main character; I thought I had to lead us all, like Amira did. But in the end I understood: it was about working together for something better. We don't all have to be leaders. Often the most brilliant people stand back and let others shine.

I realized, as things went on, that I didn't need to do it all myself. Not when I had my friends by my side, and our *jinn* to guide us.

But if you remember, stories never start at the beginning. They never stop at the end either. Our job is done, for now, but yours has just begun.

We restored the balance of our world, and tamed the four rogue *jinn*. They're free, now, to find their own human. Magic doesn't just exist in the Sahar Peninsula, after all.

It exists everywhere, to those who are willing to welcome it.

Turn the page. Go on give it a go.

Are you ready? It's your turn now. What story will you write?

THE END